A BROTHER'S OBSESSION

CHRISTOPHER COATES

Chapter 1

THE YOUNG MAN WITH NEARLY SHOULDER-LENGTH BLOND HAIR sat behind the wheel of an older silver Toyota sedan in a small parking lot on the outskirts of Tucson, Arizona.

The lot was away from homes and businesses and was where hikers parked so they could explore the desert trails.

As he waited, he watched as the sun started to rise. He'd fantasized about this day for several years, and today he was finally ready.

His heart rate increased because of the excitement of what he had planned. He'd already been parked here for close to 30 minutes, and his anticipation was almost uncontrollable. Mumbling to himself, he repeatedly tapped on the steering wheel, his anxiety needing a release.

While waiting, he imagined who the next person to park would be. Male or female, old or young, it didn't matter; he just wanted to begin.

Six minutes later, a small blue Ford pickup truck pulled in and parked at the far end of the small packed-dirt lot, bringing a smile to the man's face.

A man in his mid-thirties stepped out of the truck and casually walked toward the hiking trail, inserting earbuds as he went. The newcomer didn't look familiar, but that made no difference.

The younger man climbed out of the sedan and put on an old green ball cap. He slipped on a tan vest with large, bulging pockets and took the small, camouflaged backpack from the front floorboard. He opened it and removed three items. The first was a strange-looking pistol that he tucked into the rear of his pants, the second a two-foot-long metal tube, and lastly, a stopwatch that he hung by its cord around his neck.

Moving rapidly, with his barely perceptible limp not slowing him down, he pursued the man who'd already moved out of view on the trail. He soon had the man in sight again and moved along as quickly and silently as possible.

The dirt path had a few hills and turns. Buried rocks were sticking up a few inches in places, creating trip hazards if a hiker wasn't paying attention. A few feet off the trail, a dozen or more species of cacti grew, some well over 150 years old. As he walked, he took out the odd gun and screwed the long tube to the end, giving the handgun a crazy-looking two-foot barrel. Next, he reached into his vest pocket and took out a device that resembled a two-way radio but with six antennae coming out of the top. As soon as he flipped the switch, the cellular jammer began emitting powerful radio signals on many frequencies that were strong enough to disrupt all cellular and radio devices in the immediate area.

He watched with satisfaction as the hiker slowed, took out his temporarily impaired phone and pondered its useless state.

Because of the earbuds his quarry wore, the young man was able to get within 20 feet before being detected – well within the range of the tranquilizer gun, which he was already aiming.

Before the hiker could turn, the man pulled the trigger, and the pressurized CO_2 cartridge fired the four-inch dart, which flew 20 feet to the unsuspecting man.

Designed to deliver medication to cattle, the needle easily

penetrated the man's T-shirt and delivered its payload into the trapezius muscle in his upper back.

The assailant watched as the projectile hit its mark, pleased at how smoothly his attack had gone. As the hiker flailed around, reaching for the dart in his back, he reloaded the gun, certain another dose wouldn't be needed but wanting it ready, just in case.

"What'd you do? What's this?" the now-terrified hiker yelled while holding up the expended dart.

The attacker smiled inwardly, feeling victory approaching. He remained silent as his victim continued yelling at him and then again looked at his useless phone. Now it was simple, stay out of reach until his target dropped, then the critical part of the plan would begin.

Stepping off the trail, the pursuer, holding the tranquilizer gun, gave his victim room to return the way he'd come, should he choose to do so.

The hiker yelled some more and then sprinted back in the direction of his truck, choosing not to confront the man who was still pointing a weapon at him. As he headed towards the parking lot, he passed his assailant, who allowed him to continue by.

As the target fled, hurrying towards his car, the man with the tranquilizer gun realized he'd forgotten something and reached for the stopwatch dangling around his neck. He'd intended to start the timer as soon as he fired. He wanted an idea of how long it took for the drug to incapacitate its victim. But, in the excitement, he'd forgotten. Mentally chastising himself, he started it now, deciding to add 10 seconds to the final time. He returned to the trail and followed the man, grinning as he saw him begin weaving and then drop.

Quickly approaching, he paused the stopwatch, seeing it had been only about a minute since he'd fired the gun. He knew the dart had delivered a lethal dose of the drug, so he needed to complete his task before death took the man.

Rolling his prey so that he faced up, the man saw his victim's eyes rolled back in his head. His target was still breathing, but it was slow and shallow, so he knew he needed to hurry. Setting the pistol on the ground at his side, he removed a full-size spray can from his vest's oversized pocket. With an ear-to-ear grin, he popped off the cap. He pulled off a four-inch, L-shaped tube he'd attached to the side of the can with a rubber band and screwed it on to the short stub sticking out of the top of the can.

As he completed this, he heard a gasp and the words, "Oh no! What happened?"

Startled, he jerked his head up and, to his horror, he saw a petite African-American woman jogging up, dressed in a tank top with shorts and running shoes.

Quick to improvise, the shooter said, "Hurry! He collapsed. Give me a hand."

The woman approached, and he concealed the spray can between his victim's arm and body.

"What can I do?" the jogger asked.

Grabbing the pistol at his side, he aimed at her approaching thigh and fired. She was less than 10 feet away, but in his haste, he missed her flesh and instead hit the fanny pack she wore near her hip. The dart injected its deadly contents harmlessly into the pack.

Confused but recognizing the danger, the jogger turned and sprinted back toward her car.

Cursing, the man sprang to his feet and took off in pursuit. The situation was getting out of control and he needed to fix it fast. He reloaded the tranquilizer gun as he ran. This was the last dart he'd brought, so he needed to make it count.

Having been a sprinter in school, he caught up before the parking lot was in sight and fired into the back of her leg, causing her to stagger as she received the full dose of the deadly substance.

When she stumbled, the killer moved to get in front of her and point the now empty pistol at her.

In a state of near panic and being unfamiliar with weapons, all the woman knew was that she had a gun pointed at her, and she stopped running.

As she instinctively pulled the empty dart out of her leg, he said, "No talking. Now turn around and go back to the guy on the ground."

Even though partly winded, he managed to keep his voice calm and controlled.

"Why are you doing this? What was in this thing?" She asked with terror in her voice as she held the empty dart up.

Staying calm and using the most menacing voice he could manage, he answered, "If you don't want to get shot again, stop talking and head back."

Following his instructions, she turned around and made it about halfway back before her gait changed and she started weaving.

Seeing this, he took his concern off her and sprinted back to his first victim. Reaching the man's side, he glanced back and saw the woman face-down on the path. He allowed himself to relax. The crisis seemed under control for the moment.

The fear that someone else might come up the path almost made him give up and flee back to his car. But this morning's effort had been too long in coming, and his obsession with what he was doing forced him to carry on

Retrieving the spray can from where he'd set it, the assailant stuffed the rigid tube attached to the top of the can several inches into the man's left nostril and squeezed the trigger. As he did, he realized something was wrong. The man had already stopped breathing.

As the can began expelling its contents, the high-expansion insulating foam rushed into the man's nose, filling the sinus cavity and nasopharynx. Immediately the foam began rapidly expanding to 50 times its original volume and soon blossomed out of the mouth and other nostril.

He withdrew the tube, leaving the can about half full. Feeling for the pulse in the man's neck, he realized he'd been too late. The man died from the overdose before he could complete the most crucial part of his plan.

Seething in anger, he looked up the path at the woman. Maybe he could still salvage the morning.

Gathering his tranquilizer gun and spray can, he raced to the woman and found that she wasn't breathing but still had a faint pulse.

Reaching into his vest pocket, he removed a box about the size of a deck of cards. He ripped off the top, exposing the Narcan auto-injector. He'd brought the Narcan in case he accidentally came in contact with the deadly opioid in the darts. Taking the auto-injector out of the box, he removed the orange safety tab and pressed the device firmly against her thigh. A small needle popped out and injected the 4mg dosage, which was intended to revive people from life-threatening narcotic overdoses.

He waited a few seconds and again felt for her pulse. It was gone. The Narcan had been too little, too late. In a fury, he grabbed the spray can and repeated the process he'd used on the man, knowing the futility of his efforts.

As his customary self-disgust returned, he gathered his items and stormed back to his car. He ripped the stopwatch off and hurled it at a large rock, watching it shatter into hundreds of pieces. While walking he chastised himself. "Stupid, stupid Evan. You did it all wrong!"

Chapter 2

DETECTIVE DAN FELTY AND HIS PARTNER MACKENZIE (MAC) Bell descended the rear outside stairs of the Tucson Police Department's midtown office. The two headed toward their unmarked, department-issued SUV. It was early morning, and each carried a freshly filled, reusable coffee cup as they walked.

In his early forties, Dan was clean-shaven, six feet tall and athletic. He'd been on the force for 12 years, six of them as a detective. Mackenzie was newer to the team but still had several years of experience. She was short but extremely fast. Even with her smaller legs, Mac could outrun most of her peers. She had shoulder-length brunette hair, which she tended to wear pulled back while at work.

The pair had been partners for three years and were good friends. Today, both wore light-blue department-issued polo shirts embroidered with the Tucson Police logo on the front.

"Just once, it would be nice to sit down and make some progress on yesterday's backlog before getting called out again," Mac grumbled.

"The more you keep wishing for that, the more you'll be disappointed," her partner responded with a smile.

The detectives got into the SUV and, with Dan at the wheel, headed away from the station house.

"Two people down on a trail at this time of day. I'm glad it's early and not too hot yet," Mac added.

Teasing, Dan said, "See, that's a much better attitude. Look at the positive side of things."

Giving her partner a sarcastic glance, Mac added, "You want positive? I bet the victims were outside all night and are half-eaten by critters."

Laughing, Dan nodded. "Usually, I'll try to have a more positive attitude, but in this case, I wouldn't be surprised if you're right."

They drove the rest of the way in silence, drinking their coffee.

Approaching, they saw the small lot was packed with vehicles. Several civilian cars were present. There was also a fire engine and a large red rescue vehicle from the Tucson Fire Department. Two ambulances and four marked police SUVs, as well as a crime-scene unit and a van with the medical examiner's logo also occupied the limited space.

"Looks like everyone came out to play today," Mac commented.

"I see the district supervisor's vehicle, so try to behave."

Smiling, she replied, "Who, me? I'm always a good girl."

"Whatever!" Dan responded, laughing.

Leaving their vehicle, Dan and Mac headed to the trailhead. Yellow crime-scene tape blocked off the mouth of the trail, and a group of their colleagues approached from down the path. Five people were helping guide a yellow ambulance stretcher. Walking up, they could see the situation was more significant than the original message about two people down on the trail suggested.

The person on the stretcher wore the familiar uniform of the Tucson Police Department.

The detectives could see an endotracheal tube coming out

of the man's mouth and attached to a blue Ambu bag. The medic by the head of the stretcher squeezed the bag every few seconds to assist their patient's breathing. Another of the medics was carrying a bag of IV fluid. The tubing from the bag connected to a catheter in the officer's hand.

Seeing a fellow officer critically injured immediately changed the detectives' attitudes.

The final member of the approaching group saw them and waved them over.

Lieutenant Miller was a good leader and the detectives appreciated his attitude and the support he gave his team. He was a tall African-American with almost 25 years in the department.

Dan spoke first, "What's going on, Lieutenant?"

"You guys sure picked up an interesting one. It's the craziest thing I've ever seen. There are two bodies up the trail. Their mouths and noses are full of some kind of hard stuff. It looks like dense Styrofoam to me. When the first units arrived, Officer Hernandez went to look for ID in the woman's fanny pack. There was a big dart buried into the side of it. He removed it and reached inside. The inside of the pack was soaked in some liquid substance. It probably came out of the dart and got all over his hand.

"About three minutes later, he started having problems, and someone called for another ambulance. By the time it got here, Hernandez had collapsed. Other responders gave him Narcan, and he came around for a minute but soon went out again. EMS arrived by then, and the medics Narcaned him through the IV, and he came around, but he still went out again. They ended up intubating him because his breathing kept stopping."

"Is he going to be okay?" Mac asked, the concern in her voice evident.

"Not sure yet. We need to know what he was dosed with and what happened to those two up the trail. The crime scene unit is almost done, but I told the ME not to take the bodies until you get a look at them."

With raised eyebrows, Dan answered, "Interesting. We'll go check it out."

As the detectives headed up the trail, the lieutenant called out, "Wear gloves. We don't need any more incidents from that liquid."

"Got it," Mac called back.

"You always want the unusual ones," Dan told his partner.

"This sure sounds like it'll be interesting," she agreed.

The detectives walked a couple of hundred yards before they saw activity. Police and fire personnel stood around a body on the ground. She was a petite dark-skinned female dressed in a tank top and running shorts.

The crime-scene tech and a patrol officer walked up to meet them as they approached. Both looked familiar, but neither detective could place a name to the men.

"Morning, detectives," the officer said.

Nodding, Mac replied, "The LT says you have an interesting one for us."

"You can say that again," the crime scene tech said, handing a clear evidence bag to the detective. Inside was a four-inch-long dart that looked like a 10cc syringe with tail fins on one end and an inch-and-a-half-long needle on the other.

He explained, "The victim had this sticking out of a fanny pack. The fanny pack is already on the way to the lab in a hazmat bag."

"Any other darts?" Dan asked.

"No, but the victims have puncture wounds which possibly came from them. The shooter must have taken any other darts when he left but missed this one," the tech explained.

"How long does the ME think she's been down?" Dan asked.

"Not long. Rigor mortis hasn't started to set in, and she is still fairly warm. Probably less than an hour."

Walking up to the woman on the ground, Mac gasped, "What am I looking at?"

What she saw was much worse than expected, based on Lieutenant Miller's description.

The woman lay on her back and her neck was grossly bulging. A tennis-ball-size mass of yellow dried foam protruded from her mouth, which was open unnaturally wide. More of the foam had collected under her nostrils where it had come out of her severely stretched-out nose.

"I think I know the answer," the uniformed officer said. "What you're looking at is insulating spray foam. It comes in a spray can and is used to insulate and fill cracks and gaps. When sprayed out, it rapidly begins expanding when in contact with oxygen. It'll grow 50 times its original size in seconds. I think someone sprayed it down their throats."

"You mean that's one solid piece?" Dan asked.

"Almost certainly. The medics couldn't remove it. As it dried, it expanded. That's why her nose and throat are so swelled," the crime-scene tech added.

Dan appraised the officer. "You seem quite familiar with this stuff," he said.

"I am. I've used it before. There are several brands available that do the same thing. I've only been on the department for about a year. Before then, I worked and lived in upstate New York. I've used it several times. It does a great job of keeping cold and drafts out."

"Who would need that kind of insulation here in Arizona?" Mac asked.

"It can be used for more than insulating against cold air. It can seal holes where insects or rodents get into a building, fill cracks in cement or do a bunch of other things. It's available in hardware stores here. I've seen it," the officer explained.

Both detectives crouched down, examining the now-solid foam.

"Well, this would be a horrible way to die," the female detective said.

"Not so fast, detective," the crime-scene tech cautioned.

"What?" Mac asked.

"The guy with the ME's office noticed something. Look at her eyes."

Dan, still kneeling, shifted his focus higher on the face. "There's no petechial hemorrhaging. The eyes look fine," he noted.

"Exactly. It's the same with the other victim. Both were dead before he sprayed the foam in. If they'd suffocated on the foam, we'd see the ruptured blood vessels in the eyes," the tech said.

Looking at the evidence technician, Mac asked, "Did you find anything else of interest?"

"Just this."

He handed over another evidence collection bag. It contained a scrap of thin white cardboard that had been ripped off a small box. Most of the wording was incomplete, but the pink letters spelling out the word Narcan were legible.

"Where'd you find this?" Dan asked.

"Here next to the woman."

"Are we sure it wasn't from any of the responders?" Mac asked.

The officer spoke up, "I double-checked, and they package ours differently. The only time we used any was on Hernandez, and he was down by the male victim. Also, there's another small puncture on her thigh. Possibly caused by an auto-injector."

Confused by the situation, Mac asked, "Are there surveillance cameras in the parking lot or on the trail?"

The officer replied, "While waiting for you to get here, I called the city to check, and no. They plan to install some this year but haven't gotten to it yet."

Dan paused, trying to put the pieces of the puzzle

together in his head. Finally, he said to the others, "Anyone have any ideas? None of this makes much sense."

The man from the crime lab said, "No, none of this makes sense, but our guys found a smashed stopwatch back the way we came. It's a couple of yards off the trail. We'll get it to the lab for analysis. Not sure if it is related to the victims or not."

"Okay, let us know if you find anything else. Does anyone else have any ideas?" Dan asked.

When no one suggested anything, the detectives headed down the trail toward the other body.

Chapter 3

Evan Brown fought to control his rage as he drove. His throat felt raw, and his hands hurt from pounding them on the steering wheel as he screamed in frustration. He'd been infuriated since heading back to his car in the parking lot at the hiking trail.

He'd spent months perfecting his plans until he was sure he had everything accounted for. This morning he'd been ready, and then it had all fallen apart.

Taking the two lives had calmed his urge but only to a degree. As with the animals he'd experimented on, sitting back and watching them gasping for their final breath was what he needed to feel at peace. Today should've been his chance with an actual human subject.

Part of him was furious the female jogger had chosen that moment to come down the trail. One minute more, and he would've been done. The other part of him suspected her arrival didn't change the outcome much. His initial victim had barely been breathing before the woman arrived. His plan might have still been a failure.

Throughout the planning, he'd been concerned about using carfentanil because of how potent it was. But he needed his targets to go down quickly. He couldn't afford even a slim chance that they might get away.

Fortunately, he had a plan B. Evan always had a plan B. It had some risks, but it still should work.

His car left the main road and then traveled along several smaller streets before turning into his driveway.

Evan lived alone in a small, rundown rental house where he enjoyed the peace and quiet that desert living offered. The house was isolated, with his nearest neighbor almost a half-mile away. He'd lived here since leaving college and moving to the area almost three years before.

Getting out of his car, Evan headed inside, carrying his equipment. He set the dart pistol on the counter and plugged in the cell phone jammer to recharge.

He had converted one of the home's small bedrooms into a workroom and he headed there next. He opened the wooden cabinet mounted on the wall, removed a new package of three blue-finned darts, and set them on the white plastic folding table he'd set up under the cabinet.

Returning to the cabinet, he took out a small vial, looked at the label, and saw the word carfentanil. Understanding that this was the drug that had failed him this morning, he put it back and took out another vial. This one was twice the size, and he looked at the label and nodded. This time, things would be different. Checking the clock, he smiled and filled three darts from the new vial. Retrieving the jammer, Evan headed back to his car. He didn't have to be at work until 3 pm, so there was still time to try again. If he was a little late to work, he wasn't concerned. They'd never fire him. No one else wanted to do his job.

Chapter 4

THE PLASTIC TUBE SLID IN, AND THE TRIGGER WAS PULLED. The light yellow insulating foam spewed from the tube connected to the can and into the narrow opening, rapidly expanding. In seconds, the foam insulation pushed all the air from the available space.

Those who'd gathered watched as Detective Dan Felty released the trigger and saw the foam pouring out of the narrow opening at the mouth of the two-liter soda bottle. He'd planned to fill the bottle only halfway, but the thick goo began expanding so quickly that it overflowed the bottle before he could remove the tube.

Mac bent down and touched some of the still-expanding mass.

"It's very thick and sticky," she said.

About a dozen of their peers observed the experiment in the back lot of the Midtown Detective Bureau. Everyone on duty had heard about the bizarre call earlier in the morning and was curious about what had happened and why.

After about 20 seconds, the foam stopped expanding, and there was as much out of the bottle as inside.

Mac touched it again. "It's no longer as sticky and it's getting rigid."

"And your guy filled someone's throat with that stuff?" a watching officer asked.

"Yeah, he did," Mac answered. "Even if someone were conscious, this stuff is so thick they would've choked on it."

A voice in the audience asked, "So, what's the purpose of your experiment?"

As Detective Felty started to reply, his phone went off, signaling a text message. He noticed Mac had got the same text, so he ignored the phone and answered the question, "We weren't familiar with spray insulation and wanted an idea of what we were dealing with."

"Any suggestions on what EMS should do if they find someone with this stuff blocking their mouth and nose?" another voice inquired.

Dan shook his head as Mac spoke. "Maybe the ME will have some thoughts we can share with EMS. We're headed there next."

Looking at her partner, she added, "They're ready to see us. The ME wants us on-site, not on a video call."

Dan picked up the bottle and handed it to one of the officers in the crowd so it could be passed around.

As the detectives headed to the car, Dan said, "What do you think?"

"The test using the bottle was interesting, but seeing how it expanded doesn't help me understand why he did this. Did he know his victims? Were they random? Will there be more attacks? Was the foam a message after he killed them? Still no answers," Mac said.

Several minutes later, Dan and Mac arrived at their destination and headed into the medical examiner's office, a location with which they were all too familiar.

Their credentials gained them access to the old three-story

building, and the pair waited while the receptionist paged the examiner assigned to their case.

Dr. Emily Bonter arrived a few minutes later and motioned for the detectives to follow her. She was of medium height with short blonde hair and wore blue scrubs and a white lab coat.

"Why is it when I see something weird, I always know it'll be you two assigned to it?" she asked good-naturedly.

"What can we say, Emily? We're more interesting than most of the others," Mac responded.

Chuckling, Dr. Bonter nodded. "Well, in this case, that sure is true. That's why I wanted you here instead of on a video call."

Walking down a corridor, they entered Exam Room 6.

Mac's nose crinkled involuntarily when she entered the room as the subtle smell of disinfectant and bodily substances hit her. The brightly lit room was always a little too cold for her comfort.

The two victims from the early morning's events were stripped naked and on stainless steel exam tables with plain white sheets respectfully covering them from the chest down.

Dr. Bonter explained, "This is all preliminary. I haven't had a chance to complete the full autopsies yet, but I don't expect to find much other than what I'm about to show you. However, the few things I have so far are quite interesting."

Gathering around the male victim, she continued, "This is Colin Dandry. First, look at these X-rays of the head and neck."

An X-ray was visible on the large wall-mounted monitor screen and it showed a single light-colored mass that occupied much of the head and almost all of the neck.

Emily explained, "This is a single piece of dried foam, which expanded, taking up all the space. Then it created the deformities by pressing against all the surrounding tissues when there was no place for it to go and it still was expanding.

It extends a couple of inches into the trachea, headed toward the lungs and halfway down the esophagus toward the stomach.

"I watched a couple of videos online about spray insulation. As it expands, it will follow the path of least resistance.

"Eventually, it grew so much that it couldn't move any more and started expanding outward, causing all the swelling in the neck and face."

"I picked up some of this stuff at the store to examine, and it would have fully swelled in 30 seconds or less," Dan added.

"Your experiment matches what I saw on the video," the doctor agreed.

"Can you get it out?" Mac asked.

"Not in a single piece. I'd have to completely destroy the face and neck. I can chip away at it a little at a time, but that'd be very time-consuming, and I'm not sure what we'd learn. I'll let the mortician remove it if they choose to. I did chip off a small piece and sent it to the lab. Maybe they can identify the brand of foam the attacker used."

"We were asked to find out what EMS should do if they encounter another one of these situations," Mac said.

Emily thought for a second and answered, "The foam will completely obstruct their airways and isn't removable. It would undoubtedly be rigid by the time EMS arrived, and digging it out would take too long. Since there are only a couple of minutes where someone can survive with no oxygen, the only option I can think of is performing a cricothyrotomy.

"The paramedics would have to cut here on the cricothyroid membrane and insert a tube." As she spoke, she pointed to the place on the throat where a surgical incision would need to be made.

"If the foam had not gone too far down the trachea, this might work. In Colin's case, it's too far down, but on the woman, it isn't, and the procedure might have worked if performed quickly enough. I know the medics are trained for this, but I doubt many have ever had a reason to do it. Other than that, there isn't anything they can do. Also, the chances that the medics would be close enough to get there within only a couple minutes of the foam being applied is almost impossible."

They silently contemplated the information for a few seconds, and Dr. Bonter spoke again. "Another interesting thing is, I know what drug they used in the darts. The toxicology shows a massive dose of pure medical-grade carfentanil."

"Is carfentanil the same thing as fentanyl?" Dan inquired.

"As potent and dangerous as fentanyl is, carfentanil is a hundred times more potent. Ten thousand times stronger than morphine. They use it to sedate elephants and other large animals in the wild. It's been showing up on the streets in addicts recently and is so strong that it gets cut a thousand times or more. The dose these two received was pure and quite lethal," the doctor explained.

"Why would someone use a dose so potent?" Mac asked.

Dr. Emily explained, "A dart is an effective method of delivering medication. However, contrary to what you see on TV, when a person or animal is tranquilized with a dart gun, using an appropriate dose, the medication goes into the muscle. It takes effect much slower than if injected directly into the bloodstream. Therefore it can take 10 to 15 minutes for the animal to drop.

"The way to speed the process up is to use a larger dose or a more potent drug. My guess is your guy wanted them down more quickly than a survivable dosage would allow. Either he didn't care if they survived, or his calculation of how much of the drug to use was way off."

The detectives pondered this for a minute, then Dan asked, "When you consider the carfentanil and the foam together, any thoughts as to his intent?"

The doctor chuckled. "I think those deductions are your area of expertise, not mine."

"Yeah, that's true, but we aren't getting a good picture of what he's doing. Clearly, he wants to take them down alive, otherwise, why not shoot them with a regular gun?" Dan said.

Mac nodded. "So that suggests he wanted his victims alive when he used the foam."

"That didn't happen. They were dead, or at least not breathing when the foam was sprayed in," Dr. Bonter said.

"Exactly," Dan replied. "This means that whatever he was trying to accomplish was a failure."

"Which means he's probably going to try again," Mac deduced.

Chapter 5

TWELVE-YEAR-OLD BRITANY ARCHER PEDALED HER BICYCLE down Mill Street as fast as she could. She was more than 15 minutes late and annoyed. Her mother knew she was supposed to meet her friend Molly in the park at 11:30. She'd waited until Britany was about to leave the house to tell her she needed to help with some chores before she could go.

Arriving at Coleman Park, she was out of breath when she saw her friend sitting on a picnic table waiting with her phone in her hand.

"Where have you been? I've been waiting for ever," Molly said in an irritated tone.

"My mother needed me to help her move some furniture. Someone's coming today to clean the carpets. I don't know why she waited until I was headed out the door to ask."

"Whatever. Let's get going before it gets any hotter."

Britany rolled her bike to the rack, placed it next to her friend's and locked it up, using a chain with a combination lock.

Heading back to the table, she saw Molly stretching her legs and joined in. After a minute, the girls exchanged glances, nodded, and started running along the path.

The girls were part of a running team in their middle school and trained together several times each week.

As they ran, they scanned the ground, always on the lookout for a snake that might be sunning itself on the path.

After about a half mile, Molly spotted one on the edge of the trail. "Snake," she said calmly as she pointed.

Both girls recognized it as a harmless kingsnake but still veered off the path to avoid getting too close.

They continued further and were approaching some decorative bushes on the side of the trail when a man stepped out, blocking their path. He wore a ball cap and was pointing a gun at them.

The girls came to an abrupt stop.

Britany, who had done some target shooting with her uncle, noticed that the gun looked strange and had an abnormally long barrel, making her wonder if it was a real gun or a toy.

The guy holding it didn't speak. He stood as still as the girls, staring at them with a look of surprise. After a few seconds, the gun in his hand started shaking uncontrollably.

As one, the girls started to back away.

The gun was still pointed in their direction when the man collapsed to his knees and started crying.

Without speaking, the girls turned and ran, as fast as they could, back the way they'd come.

After looking back several times, Britany relaxed a little when she was sure the man wasn't chasing them.

Chapter 6

THE NEXT DAY

AFTER WORKING A LONG THIRD SHIFT AT A LOCAL manufacturing company, Ron Parker walked the paved path through Santa Cruz River Park. He lived nearby and often unwound after getting home by taking an early-morning walk. The fact that his doctor wanted him to lose 20 pounds helped his motivation each day.

Occasionally he'd see someone jogging, but that was uncommon. As for Ron, running held no interest. Walking was all the exercise his doctor would get from him.

This morning, he reached the point where the path made a sharp bend to the south. This is where he usually turned around to head home, and he noticed someone approaching. It was a male in his early to mid-twenties. He had on a dingy green baseball cap without wording and was looking at the ground.

The guy seemed to be ignoring Ron, so he didn't bother greeting the man. A few steps after they passed each other, Ron felt a stabbing pain in his buttock. He whipped around at the same time as he reached for the source of the pain.

He felt something sticking in through his shorts and yanked it out. It was a four-inch-long blue-finned dart. A needle was on one end, and the body of the dart looked like a syringe. Ron could see the syringe was empty. The payload was already moving through his body.

Ron took several steps forward as his attacker frantically worked to reload the weapon. As he was about to strike, the man finished and brought the weapon up, aiming at Ron's chest.

Ron stopped and froze, "What was it? What did you shoot me with?"

"If you don't want to get shot again, stand still and calm down. The dose you got isn't fatal, but another will be," the assailant said.

"What was it?" Ron screamed while taking a step back.

"Shut up and stand still." The man jabbed the long-barrelled tranquilizer pistol in Ron's direction.

Ron had read online about what had happened the day before and realized the man was trying to delay him until whatever was in the dart took effect. He wasn't sure if the dose he'd gotten was lethal but believed the man when he said the next dart would add enough that it would be. If he ran, he was sure he'd be shot in the back.

Pulling out his phone, Ron was confused to see he had no service.

"Your phone won't work," the attacker calmly said.

Not understanding, Ron put the phone away.

For over a minute, he stood there pleading with the man who held the pistol to let him go. Then Ron became aware of a strange feeling developing and knew he was running out of time. With the empty dart still gripped in his left hand, Ron dodged to his right, and the pistol fired, the dart missing him by almost a foot. Less than two seconds later, he reached his assailant.

Ron's first punch struck the center of the face, smashing the man's nose. The second struck near the left eye, and the attacker dropped.

The lethargy rapidly increased as his exertion did and Ron knew he was in big trouble. It was more than a half-mile back to his neighborhood. However, the trail he was on paralleled the highway, and Ron could hear traffic noise. Ron took off at a sprint, off the trail and across the desert, rapidly covering the brief distance toward the expressway.

After almost a minute, the sluggishness nearly overwhelmed him as the traffic flowing by came into view. In his compromised state, he lost his footing and fell. His shoulder brushed against a short cactus with half-inch-long needles. Ron screamed, the pain briefly reducing the drug's effect. He clumsily got back to his feet and continued running, with sweat now soaking him. As he approached the highway, he became even more confused as the drug continued its assault on him.

Chapter 7

THE DOOR TO THE HOUSE OPENED AND TWIN 13-YEAR-OLD girls raced out, laughing as they headed to their mother's white sedan. By the time their mother left the single-story house, her daughters were already in the car, and the doors were closing.

Connie Douglas got in the driver's seat and smiled as she looked in the mirror at her daughters, who were in an abnormally good mood for so early in the day.

Backing out of the driveway, she headed towards the junior high school, as she did each morning.

Once at the school, the car had barely stopped when the back doors burst open, and the girls hopped out, shouting a quick, "Bye, mom," as the doors shut again.

The girls had both been unusually cooperative this morning. Because of this, Connie was running a little ahead of schedule and decided to treat herself to a mocha latte from her favorite drive-through coffee shop instead of waiting to get the mediocre free coffee in the office.

With her beverage in hand, she merged on to the six-lane divided highway, pleased with how the day had started. She turned up the radio a little and sang along to a familiar song as she drove.

The highway was busy but moving at a steady pace. She drove in the right lane holding the 20oz cup in her hand, its contents still too hot to drink.

Connie became aware of brake lights ahead. Some of the cars were attempting to move out of the right lane. Seconds later, she saw why. A man was standing near the edge of the highway. He was only about 20 yards ahead and dressed in shorts and a T-shirt. He staggered with something clutched in his right hand and appeared intoxicated. She started to move to the left and realized the semi-truck next to her blocked her escape. She tried to slow down but was still going 50mph when the man stumbled forward directly in front of her.

It happened so suddenly that she didn't have time to react.

The impact was jarring, and because the pedestrian was staggering and slumped, he didn't come up on to the hood but went down under the wheels.

In that moment of horror, Connie unconsciously squeezed the coffee cup crushing the flimsy container and soaking her arm and right leg with scalding liquid.

Screaming in pain and terror and unaware of all the blowing horns and squealing breaks, Connie side-swept the truck to her left. The sound of grinding metal got her attention back to her situation, and she regained control and got her car stopped on the right shoulder.

By the time she got out of her car, shaking as she walked, all the traffic had stopped.

Chapter 8

DAN AND MAC STARTED THEIR MORNING BY LOOKING AT DR. Emily Bonter's notes from the ME's office.

The full autopsies had been completed in the night, and the reports awaited the detectives upon their arrival today. As expected, the examinations of the two victims from the previous day were unremarkable except for what they already knew.

"Well, there's nothing here of any interest," Mac noted.

"Good. We don't need another factor to consider," Dan answered.

As the detectives were chatting, Lieutenant Miller stepped out of his office and called out, "Can I get your attention!" He paused while half a dozen conversations in the room ended. "I just heard that Officer Hernandez is expected to recover fully. The doctors needed to maintain his vitals until the drug wore off. Still, he's now awake, alert, and will probably be discharged this evening."

Loud cheering erupted, continuing for several seconds, then the lieutenant continued, "Felty and Bell, I need to see you in my office."

The duo entered their lieutenant's office and closed the door.

"What's up, LT?" Dan asked.

"A few minutes ago, I got off the phone with detective George Jenkins from the Pima County sheriff's department. There was another incident yesterday. A pair of teen girls were jogging on a path in a park just outside the city limits. A man approached them and pulled out a strange-looking pistol. They ran away before he could shoot and didn't get a good look at him. After looking at some photos, they identified the gun as a pistol used to shoot tranquilizer darts into livestock.

"I gave Detective Jenkins your numbers. If this was the same guy, I want you to share information with the sheriff's department," the lieutenant said.

Dan nodded. "Not a problem. We've interacted with them before. They're good to work with."

Mac nodded her agreement.

Miller responded, "He'll be calling sometime this morning. Now, I have something else for you. I need you to get out to I-19, South of I-10. There's a pedestrian struck on the highway. Officers on the scene think it might be related to your incident yesterday."

Heading back to their desks, Dan and Mac logged out of their computers and headed out after refilling their coffee cups.

Because of the morning traffic, it took the detectives more than 15 minutes to arrive on the scene. They had to drive the last mile on the highway's shoulder. The patrol officers had gotten one of the three lanes moving. But traffic was still backed up and crawling as drivers strained to get a look at what was happening around all the emergency vehicles.

When they arrived, the detectives saw a well-dressed woman in her late thirties talking to paramedics. She was holding an ice pack against her forearm and was crying.

The patrol sergeant, Chris Katten, approached them. "Morning, detectives."

"Hey Chris, what do you have?" Dan said.

"From what the witnesses say, the victim stumbled along the shoulder and went into traffic. It sounds like at least three cars ran him over."

Wearing a curious expression, Mac asked, "You think this is related to yesterday's dart-gun case?"

The sergeant handed Mac an evidence bag. Inside were the broken remains of a tranquilizer dart. It was identical to the one recovered the day before. "Witnesses who saw him on the shoulder before he stepped into the traffic say he was holding something in his hand and he was moving as if drugged. We recovered this from the roadway. It looks like it went flying when the first car struck him, and it was run over several times.

"He left footprints in the dirt as he stumbled along. I sent two officers to follow them back so we can try to locate where he was drugged."

Nodding in the direction of the covered body lying on the roadway, Dan asked, "Did you see a wound left by the dart?"

"Nothing obvious on the front of the body. The crime-scene techs are still getting photos. When ready, they'll roll him over and check his backside."

While talking, a voice came across the sergeant's radio, "Two-six from three-two."

"Go ahead, three-two," Sergeant Katten answered.

"We tracked the victim about 75 yards to a hiking trail. There's blood on the ground. It looks like there was a fight here. Can you send the crime-scene guys to me?" the voice on the radio asked.

As Sergeant Katten went to give instructions to the crime-scene team, Dan said to his partner, "Your choice, Mac. Talk to the witnesses or head over to where the fight happened?"

"You can talk to the witnesses. I'll walk out with the tech and check out what the officer found," she answered.

As she walked away from the highway, Mac noticed a disturbance in the dirt by a small barrel cactus. It looked like someone had fallen into it, and she cringed, imagining what that would have felt like.

Mac continued for several minutes, noting the uneven steps taken by the victim and staying several yards to the left of the path he took, following in the steps of the officers who had preceded her. She doubted the footprints would be of value but didn't want to disturb any possible evidence.

When she reached the trail, she approached the uniformed officers. "So, what did you guys find?" she asked.

A tall, blonde female officer answered, "Scuffed-up dirt and blood on the trail. It looks to me like someone was injured and lay here for a while before leaving. That blood loss wouldn't have been life-threatening."

Mac looked at the spot from several angles agreeing with the first impression.

"Did you find any more blood?" she asked.

The officer added, "We walked the trail about a hundred yards in each direction and didn't see anything. We could get a K9 officer out here to try tracking them, if you want."

Mac nodded, agreeing to the suggestion.

Chapter 9

WHEN EVAN REGAINED CONSCIOUSNESS, THERE'D BEEN NO SIGN of his target, but he heard sirens from the nearby freeway. His whole face was excruciatingly painful, and his nose was bleeding heavily. He picked up the dart gun, dripping more blood on the ground as he did so, and a wave of dizziness almost made him fall.

Next, he carefully removed his T-shirt, making sure not to catch it on his damaged face. He balled it up and pressed it gingerly against his nose. Even the gentle pressure caused the pain to intensify. While feeling nauseated and with a splitting headache, he held the shirt in place as he stumbled back to his car, careful not to leave a blood trail for the authorities to follow.

He could feel his left eye swelling shut, further intensifying his feelings of failure and self-loathing. This was his third attempt and third failure. The thoughts of suicide, which had been buried since devising his plans, returned.

He'd dosed his target successfully, but the guy had managed to do quite a bit of damage to him before running away. Evan didn't know where his target went but knew the man had seen his face. If he survived the drug he'd been shot with, he'd be able to identify him.

As he stumbled, Evan knew he had a concussion. He felt sick to his stomach and wanted to lie down until the pain subsided, but he pushed on, unwilling to be defeated. Evan used his building anger as motivation and soon saw the road ahead. He'd parked his car two streets over and got there as quickly as possible while trying not to attract attention.

Once seated in the sedan, he headed home, thinking about his latest failure. He'd put months of effort into the planning and procuring the drugs for the dart guns. But clearly, they were the plan's weakness and not necessary for the ultimate outcome. Next time he'd simplify things. There'd be no more failures. It was time for plan C and, for that, he'd need help.

Once at home, Evan struggled to get out of his car while holding his crumpled-up shirt against his mangled nose.

Inside the house, he swapped the blood-soaked shirt for a towel and tossed the shirt in the kitchen sink. He needed to rest, but he knew the throbbing in his face would keep him awake.

He headed to the bathroom and looked in the mirror. The nasal swelling was extreme, and the deformity was obvious.

He broke into a cold sweat, knowing what he was about to experience. Carefully, he grasped the bridge of the nose and yanked it straight, letting out a primordial scream. The pain was indescribable. His legs buckled, and he went down, almost smashing his face on the sink. Tears flowed as he gasped for breath, wishing he had passed out.

After several minutes on the floor, he slowly got to his feet and looked in the mirror again. His nose looked better, but Evan couldn't determine if it was now set right because of all the swelling. The blood was flowing heavily again and he inadvertently swallowed some, which increased his nausea.

He took three towels and folded them together. He'd try to sleep on his side so the blood could drain until it stopped.

Taking a gallon-sized plastic storage bag, he filled it with ice and zipped it shut. It should be large enough to cover the nose and swollen eye.

Lastly, he needed to deal with the pain, so he went to the cabinet in his workroom and took out a vial. It was the carfentanil. The temptation was huge, but Evan, while homicidal, wasn't an idiot. He knew this would be great for the pain, but it was so potent that he could easily overdose, and there wouldn't be anyone around to help him if that happened.

Reluctantly, he put the vial back in the cabinet and took out a larger one. This was the same drug that he'd used early this morning. It was still a bit extreme but was a safer option. Hopefully, he'd sleep for several hours.

Taking a 10cc syringe from the cabinet, he unwrapped it and stuck the needle into the top of the vial. He filled the syringe about a quarter of the way, then returned the vial to the cabinet.

Taking the ice and syringe to the bedroom, he sat on the side of the bed and let his left leg hang loose. It took several seconds to build up the courage, then he stabbed his leg with the needle and injected the contents.

Setting the syringe down on the nightstand, Evan positioned himself on his side with the towels under his head and the ice on his nose.

The bag of ice partially impaired his vision, but he made sure he could still see the far wall and the photos on it.

As he waited for the ketamine to take effect, he stared at the young girl in the multiple photos on the wall and wept for the person who'd led him down the dark path he was on.

Chapter 10

Mackenzie Bell sat at her desk talking on the phone with a detective with the Pima County Sheriff's Department.

"Detective Jenkins. This is Mackenzie Bell with TPD."

"Just call me George. I assume you're calling about yesterday's attack in the park?"

"That's right. We've had three people shot with tranquilizer darts in the last couple of days. All have died. I was wondering if your incident might be related," Mac said.

"I've been following your cases, and the incident we had would've been only a few hours after your first one. There were two 12-year-old girls. They're part of a school running program and were jogging together in Coleman Park. They run there together almost every day.

"Suddenly, a guy steps out of the bushes and points a long-barrelled weapon at them. We believe it was a dart pistol from the description and photos we showed them."

"Did they survive?" Mac asked with concern in her voice.

"Yea, they're fine. That's where it gets weird. The girls say as soon as the guy looked at them, he seemed surprised and scared. He just stared at them and didn't shoot. After a few seconds, his gun started shaking, and he collapsed to his knees, crying. That's when the girls turned and ran for help. By the time we got deputies there, he was long gone."

After a few seconds to think, Mac said, "Were they able to give you a description of the guy?"

"Nothing reliable, other than the gun. One of the girls said he was young, and the other said he was older. They do agree he had on a ball cap, but one thought it was blue, and the other said green."

"Did he say anything to them?"

"When he was crying, he said something, but they couldn't understand what it was. Nothing else."

"Did you find any evidence at the scene?"

"Nothing. The girls were quite scared and aren't even exactly sure where on the trail this happened."

"So, George, what were your impressions of what happened?" Mac asked.

"If I had to guess, this guy was waiting for his victim to come along and jumped out when he heard the girls. I don't think he was expecting kids."

"I guess we're lucky he doesn't want to shoot kids."

George Jenkins said, "There is more to this than just not wanting to shoot kids. If it was just that, and the wrong target came along, his reaction to them wouldn't have been to collapse crying. There was something more. Maybe he has kids of his own, maybe not. But they triggered something in him."

"Yeah, I would agree with that. Did you learn anything else?" Mac asked.

"No, nothing," Jenkins said. "What about the attacks you've had? Mind sharing the details?"

Mac spent 10 minutes filling George Jenkins in on the investigation. When they disconnected, they agreed to keep each other informed of any new developments.

When she hung up, she noticed Dan watching her with interest from his desk that butted up to hers.

As Mac was filling him in on her conversation with the detective from the sheriff's department, a message popped up on her screen asking if she had time for a quick meeting. Before she could type a reply, her partner did from his computer, stating they'd both be available in two minutes.

"Mac, did you see the message from Emily?" Dan asked.

"Yup. Let's see what she found."

Wanting to be away from the noise of all the others working in the room, the two detectives headed down the hall to the large conference room. The lights came on automatically as they entered. There was a large oval table with twelve seats, and Mac took the one by a computer permanently installed on the table. Soon the 60-inch wall-mounted computer monitor lit up. They could see Dr. Emily Bonter standing in an autopsy suite in the medical examiner's office.

A wall-mounted camera in the conference room faced the table and wirelessly connected to the computer. This allowed Emily to see everyone in the room.

"Hey, Emily. Can you hear me?" Mac asked.

"Hi, guys. I hear you fine."

Dan spoke. "Excellent. What do you know?" he inquired.

"Several things. I just finished up the preliminary assessment on Ron Parker. First, your subject is still learning and experimenting. He must have decided the carfentanil is too potent, so this time he switched to ketamine," Dr. Bonter explained.

"So, how's that different?" Dan asked.

"Ketamine is still an anesthetic and can be used on people or large animals, depending on the dose. Think about it like this – carfentanil will sedate an elephant and ketamine is often used on horses. So not as potent.

"The dose he delivered would have been close to lethal for a human, but it takes longer to take effect. This time the victim had time to fight and run, and he did fight back."

"How do you know?" Mac asked.

"When he was run over on the highway by several vehicles, he sustained many broken bones. I did a full-body X-ray, and one of the few things not damaged by traffic was his right hand, but there's a fracture in the fifth metacarpal bone. That type of fracture is often referred to as a boxer's fracture and is what we see when someone punches something extremely hard. The fracture was fresh, and I don't think it happened on the roadway. I think he punched someone a couple of times, very hard."

"We found blood at the site of the attack," Mac verified. "Maybe this guy did some damage to his attacker."

"Did you find a puncture from a dart?" Dan asked.

"Yeah, in the left buttock."

"Anything else interesting?" Mac inquired.

"I found a bunch of cactus needles in his right shoulder but nothing else. I'll let you know more when I finish the internal exam. However, I did have a thought," the medical examiner said.

"What's that?" Dan asked.

"Carfentanil is being seen on the streets occasionally. Dealers can cut it up to a thousand times to make it less lethal. So, while it's quite dangerous, there's good profit for them. However, it's difficult to obtain the pure medical grade your guy has. There just isn't much of the stuff available. Ketamine, on the other hand, is a different class of drug. One is a narcotic, and the other a sedative. The abusers of one aren't likely to use the other. The one place these medications cross paths is in large-animal veterinary medicine.

"You might want to look into veterinary pharmacies, zoos, cattle ranches, and large farms and see if they've had any break-ins reported. It isn't a certainty, but the assailant may have gotten both drugs from a single place."

Nodding, Dan said, "That's good. Real good. We'll look into where the drugs came from."

"Well, that's all I've got right now. You two go and find this guy. He's given me too much work already."

"Thanks, Emily. Let us know if you learn anything more," Mac said as she disconnected the call.

After a minute, Mac said, "If you want to look into hospitals for people coming in who may have been punched hard enough to do damage, I'll start looking into any cases of thefts of large-animal tranquilizers."

"Agreed," Dan said, glad to have a plan.

Chapter 11

Twenty-four hours later, Dan, Mac, and Lieutenant Miller were back in the conference room.

The lieutenant spoke first. "I'm sure you guys are doing all you can, but Deputy Chief Sawyer is asking for the status of this investigation. So I need to hear where things stand."

Mac answered, "We understand. Dan and I've been following up on different angles and are now coming together with what we found. After this interview, and the discussion, maybe you'll think of something we didn't."

Dan nodded his agreement. His ego could handle someone else's perspective on his work.

"Let's get started," Miller said.

Mac logged into the laptop, opened her email, and clicked on the link she'd received. As she did, she explained, "I spent the day contacting all the veterinary centers, ranches, and zoos in the area. This one is the only one that has experienced a break-in recently."

The logo for Wildwood Veterinary Services was displayed on the large wall-mounted monitor.

Seconds later, a middle-aged, balding Hispanic man

appeared on the screen. "Hello, this is Dr. Cruz," the man said.

"Hello, Doctor. I'm Detective Mackenzie Bell with the Tucson Police Department. I'm here with some of my colleagues to discuss a recent break-in reported at your facility. Your assistant confirmed the break-in for me but said you'd have the details."

The doctor nodded a greeting to the two men sitting with Mac. "That's correct. There was a robbery here a few weeks ago."

"Doctor, can you give us a brief overview of what you and your business do?" Mac asked.

"I'm the director and senior veterinarian here at Wildwood. We provide veterinary services for non-domestic animals. Our typical patients are horses, cattle, bison, and the occasional bear. We frequently go on-site to ranches and farms and occasionally assist at local zoos."

"So, you would regularly use drugs such as carfentanil and ketamine?" Dan asked.

"Ketamine for certain. Carfentanil much less often, but occasionally."

"And both were stolen in the robbery three weeks ago. Correct?" Mac verified.

"Correct. We assumed it was someone wanting to get high. That occasionally happens, even though we keep all controlled medications locked and secure. If someone wants them bad enough, they'll find a way to get to them."

"Were any other drugs taken?" Mac asked.

"Unfortunately. The thieves ripped the locked cabinet off the wall and took it with them. The report we filed with the sheriff's department has the entire list of everything taken."

"We've been in touch with the sheriff's department, and they'll send the report over. It hasn't arrived yet. If the list isn't included, will you be able to get it for me?" Mac asked.

"Yeah, if needed, we can get a copy for you. I had to

submit that complete list to the DEA. When multiple controlled substances go missing, it needs to be reported at the federal level," the director said.

"Do you recall how much of the carfentanil and ketamine was taken?" Dan questioned.

"I'd have to check the report to be sure, but I believe it was four 10ml vials of carfentanil and four 30ml vials of ketamine.

"One last question. Was anything else taken in the robbery?" Mac asked.

"One tranquilizer gun and two boxes of darts were taken, too."

Dan asked, "How many darts are in a box?"

"Twelve. Each box has four packs of three darts."

"Did the darts have blue fins?" Mac asked.

"Yes, the brand we use are blue."

The people in the conference room all looked at one another. They were convinced.

"Nothing else was taken?" Dan asked.

"Nothing that we were able to find," Dr. Cruz answered.

"What about surveillance cameras? Were there any in the area where the drugs were taken?" Lieutenant Miller asked.

"No. We didn't have any cameras in that area. We have since had some installed. The insurance company required it."

Mac glanced around the room and saw from the men's expressions that there were no other questions.

"Thank you for your time today, Dr. Cruz. Please let us know if you think of anything more. We might be in touch later if we have any more questions," Mac added.

"You know where to find me. Good luck finding this guy."

A few seconds later, Mac disconnected the session.

"Well, I guess we know where our subject got the drugs," Dan said.

The others nodded.

"Were you able to track him to any emergency rooms? We know he had injuries," Mac asked.

"No. I contacted all the area hospitals and clinics. I was able to rule out the few cases with injuries similar to what we expected. However, I had the lab rush the DNA processing on the blood found at the scene. I just forwarded the results to you."

Mac opened the file on the laptop so they could see it on the large screen.

Dan explained, "From the blood left at the last scene and the DNA analysis, we know he's a male who stands about six foot tall with brown hair and blue eyes. His blood type is O negative. The DNA suggests he's mostly of European descent with about one-eighth Native American ancestry. Therefore he's Caucasian."

Lieutenant Miller nodded. "That isn't very specific, but a lot more than you had before. Is there any other new information?"

"Actually, there is," Dan said. "Officers found a smashed stopwatch near the first scene. The final report is back; there are no finger prints and no DNA. There is nothing to tie it to the case. For all we know, it could have been out there all night. Also, we just got the lab results back on the piece of spray foam the ME sent in from the first victim. The product is called FoamX. There are many brands of spray foam, and FoamX is the market leader. It's available in almost every hardware store and major retailers. I'm not sure how much help that information will be, but we know what he's using."

Miller replied, "It's another piece of information. Good progress, guys. You two keep at this and let me know what else turns up. Also, remember to keep in touch with the detective at the sheriff's department. If I have any other suggestions, I'll let you know."

Chapter 12

EVAN WOKE WITH THE SUNLIGHT SHINING THROUGH HIS uncurtained window. Groaning, he rolled over, pushed away the blood-stained sheet, and forced himself from bed.

He'd allowed himself two days to heal, but now he had things to do and someone to meet. Also, he needed to return to work this afternoon. He'd called in several times recently and still needed his job.

The pain was still constant, and his swollen nose passed minimal air making it necessary to breathe through his mouth. Because of this, his mouth always felt dry, forcing him to drink lots of water.

While convalescing, his mood had swung between despair and rage, finally settling down as he began setting his new plans in motion.

Evan's only friend, Diego, was someone he'd met in school and he lived only about an hour away. Diego had broken with his criminal past and made something of himself. He was the reason Evan moved to the Tucson area when he had nowhere else to call home. Diego might have had a new life, but he still had family and connections on the streets of Tucson. He'd reluctantly arranged a meeting for this afternoon, and Evan wanted to arrive early. Forcing himself to take his first shower in a week, he scrubbed all the blood from his hands and arms and then did his best to clean his injured face. The swelling had gone down some but was still quite noticeable, and the pain was a constant reminder of his most recent failure.

He swallowed four ibuprofen and got dressed before going into his workroom. He opened the cabinet on the wall and ignored the eleven cans of spray foam on the large bottom shelf. Reaching to the middle shelf, he withdrew one of the three remaining vials of carfentanil. He'd used one vial several days ago. He divided it between the first three darts he fired in his first attack. Sacrificing this one would still leave him two, in the unlikely event he needed to go in that direction again.

Evan got in the silver sedan, headed into town, and stopped at a city recreational area. He parked along a side street, near a deserted baseball field. Evan got out of the car and walked down the street to the gate that allowed him access to the field. He headed to the first-base dugout and stepped inside. Examining the structure, he found where the ceiling and rear wall met. A board ran the length of the dugout, and half of it was exposed. Removing the vial from his pocket, he tucked it on the board, out of sight. The idea of making a trade with drug dealers made him uncomfortable, and he wasn't going to get ripped off.

He left the dugout and walked around the ballfield, waiting for the man he planned to meet.

Fifteen minutes later, three men approached. The trio wore tank tops and were covered in tattoos. They looked to be a little older than Evan. Probably in their mid to late twenties and of Latino heritage. One carried a small backpack. Evan was confident these were the people his friend told him to meet.

As the one in the lead approached, he snickered, "They told me to look for the guy who had a busted face. It looks like your little sister gave you quite a whopping."

His companions laughed at their leader's jibe.

Evan replied, "I figured it would be an easy way for you to know it was me. What do you have?"

"Not so fast. You're supposed to have something for me."

"I do. But first, let me see what you brought," Evan insisted.

"Don't you trust me?"

"As much as you trust me. Show me, and I'll give it to you."

"Maybe my boys here will give you another beating and just take it," the gang leader said.

"You won't get it. I stashed it here somewhere."

As he spoke, Evan made sure not to look in the direction of the dugout.

The gang leader gave Evan a disapproving glare, then smiled and shoved him on the shoulder. "I'm messing with you, gringo! We're here for an honest trade."

His men snickered.

Evan returned the smile, not believing the older man.

The leader signaled to the member of his crew carrying the backpack, who stepped forward and opened it, showing Evan the contents.

Inside, Evan saw a black-and-yellow Taser pistol and 20 replacement cartridges.

The man holding the backpack explained, "This is the good one. The same as the cops use. Not the weaker version anyone can buy."

Evan nodded and smiled. "Most important, the serial numbers on the cartridges can't be traced to me."

"That's true. What're you going to do with it?" the gang leader asked.

"You don't want to know," Evan answered.

Shrugging, the leader said, "So where's my stuff?" not yet handing the backpack over.

Pointing to the dugout, Evan said, "In here."

They walked the 20 yards to the dugout and entered. Evan reached up, and as he did, he became aware of the gang members stiffening as he reached for a hidden object.

Slowly he brought the vial down and saw them relax. He handed it over, and the leader inspected the 10ml vial of clear liquid.

"How do I know this is real?"

"The factory seal is still on the top of the vial. Once removed, it can't be replaced. Also, I'm not so stupid as to try and rip you off. My friend Diego set up this trade, and I've known him for years. I wouldn't do anything to cause him problems with you."

The leader gave Evan an appraising stare. "I don't know Diego. I work for his cousin, and he told me to get this trade done," he said, deciding he believed him.

"They told me this would stop an elephant. Is that true?" The gang member asked.

"I've never tried it on an elephant, but that's what I hear," Evan answered.

"Do you have more of it? I can't use it, but the person I work for will cut this 500 times or more."

Evan lied, "I don't have any now, but if I get more, I'll let your boss know."

The leader nodded to his subordinate, who surrendered the backpack to Evan.

Heading back to his car Evan fought to contain his excitement as the euphoria washed over him. Now he was ready to try again.

Chapter 13

LEON CONWAY DROVE FIVE MILES HOME AFTER DROPPING HIS daughter off at preschool. He and his wife Sandy had delayed having children because of their careers, and they were both now in their late thirties.

Sandy was a commercial airline pilot with an irregular schedule. It worked well that Leon ran his accounting practice out of their home and could do most of the caring for their daughter, Ashley.

He pressed the button for the garage door and waited as it rose before backing in. He made sure to leave room for his wife in case she returned before he left again. He'd long ago stopped trying to keep her schedule memorized.

Exiting the car, Leon walked to the street and grabbed the garbage can he'd heard being emptied as he made Ashley her peanut butter toast for breakfast.

As he pulled the can back to the side of the garage, he glanced at his watch, seeing he still had 15 minutes before his first video call of the morning. Leon smiled, knowing this would allow him time to get another cup of coffee before starting work.

Stepping inside, he went to the sink, washed his hands, and picked up his cup, which was still a quarter full from earlier. The cup had been a Father's Day gift and had his daughter's photo printed on it. He topped it off and headed to the bedroom that he'd converted into his office.

Leon made it halfway into the room when he noticed an uncapped spray can on the corner of the desk. A strange L-shaped tube came off the top. He approached, confused as to where the can came from. As he did, a man stepped out of the closet.

The intruder appeared to be in his early twenties and wore shorts, a T-shirt, and rubber gloves. On his head sat a dirty green ball cap. Leon thought the man might have recently been in a fight because he had a purple bruise around his left eye and swollen nose. The most interesting thing was the weapon in his hand. Leon had watched enough prime-time TV to know what a Taser looked like.

Before he could speak, the weapon fired, and hundreds of tiny confetti disks blasted outward. Called AFIDs – anti-felon identification – these pieces of confetti each had the serial number of the Taser cartridge imprinted on them. These allow law enforcement to identify the purchaser of the Taser cartridge. In this case, that system failed because the cartridges were acquired illegally from a batch stolen from a police depot.

Along with the confetti, two barbed metal darts blasted out, traveling at 180 feet per second. A 35-foot length of thin wire connected the darts to the Taser's body.

On impact, the darts embedded themselves, one in Leon's abdomen and the other in his right thigh.

Instantly 50,000 volts traveled across the wires and into Leon, disrupting his neurologic and muscular systems.

Every muscle in his body contracted with each of the 95, two-milliamp electrical pulses delivered during the five-second cycle.

As Leon dropped to the ground, almost striking his head on the desk, the coffee cup flew from his hand, dumping its contents. It landed on the carpet unbroken.

Remaining conscious, Leon couldn't move, and when he tried to speak, only a gurgling groan came out.

Chapter 14

His FINGER PULLED THE TRIGGER, AND EVAN FELT A THRILL OF excitement as he saw the barbs hit their target precisely as planned. His model of Taser had two cartridges, which fired separately. He could immediately shoot again if the first one missed, but the second wouldn't be needed today.

His target, whom he randomly chose while driving the streets in the neighborhood a few days before, collapsed into a spasming heap.

Grabbing the spray can from the desk, Evan dropped to his knees, setting the Taser by his leg where he could squeeze the trigger again if needed.

The man lay partly on his side, and Evan rolled him to his back.

He forced the tube several inches into his victim's nose, and the man tried to pull his head away, but the effort was weak and ineffective. With an ear-to-ear grin, the killer depressed the trigger, and the spray foam burst out of the nozzle and began rapidly expanding.

The man on the floor immediately started gagging, but the thickness of the foam and his body's impairment from the Taser attack were too much for him to combat it. He flopped around in an uncoordinated way, a clear look of terror on his face. Only after the foam started coming out the mouth and the other nostril did Evan release the trigger. Relaxing, he took a deep breath and studied his victim until he stopped moving, taking in every moment, burning the image into memory.

He placed two fingers on the man's neck, gently pressing against the carotid artery. He felt the pulse as it slowed and eventually stopped. Evan moved back, sitting against the wall, looking at the dead man, and felt a sense of peace wash over him.

Then his thoughts went to his sister, and he started to weep uncontrollably. After so many years, he'd finally gotten to see how his family had died – fighting to breathe air that wasn't there.

While he sat, his mind wandered back in time to the point where this had all begun.

He'd been 11 years old and was riding in the back seat of his mother's minivan, next to his little sister, Patti. This had been during the strange period when he was still getting used to being named Evan and not Blake, his birth name.

His stepfather, Ray, was driving as they headed home from his favorite pizza restaurant. It was a special treat because it was Patti's eighth birthday.

It had been a wonderful time until the adults started screaming at each other and were told to leave the restaurant.

Evan tried not to pay attention to their frequent arguments but could tell his mother wasn't happy with how much her new husband was drinking that night. Evan didn't know much about things like that, but he knew his mom had drunk as much. She'd been doing that a lot, ever since their lives had abruptly changed. Evan may have been a child, but he knew she wasn't dealing well with the drastic changes in her life.

Today's argument wasn't unusual. The drinking was one of many things they frequently fought about. But having it happen in public was uncommon. As the yelling continued on the way home, Evan had looked over at his sister Patti and saw the tears running down her face. The argument had ruined the fun birthday celebration. He reached out and took her hand, which she clutched like a lifeline.

It was sad because, when they weren't drinking, Mom and Ray were very nice, and they often did fun things together. Evan would still have preferred to be with his real father, but he knew that was impossible.

When these arguments happened at home, the children tended to seek each other out, and Evan would put on a brave front as he held his heartbroken sister, sometimes for hours.

Long ago, when this had first started, he'd promised Patti, whose name used to be Cindy, that he would always be there when she needed him, and he was determined to keep the promise.

From the curves in the road, the kids knew they were on Lakeside Drive and would soon be home.

Years later, Evan read the police report and learned the van had been going too fast and drifted into oncoming traffic. As a car approached, his stepfather jerked the wheel to the right in order to avoid a collision. But the van went off the road and rolled down an embankment several times before dropping into the lake.

Evan clearly remembered the van jerking to the right and his mom screaming in horror as they started to roll. The window next to him exploded, and with the next roll, the motion threw him from the vehicle. He struck the ground hard, bouncing and rolling several times, ending up on his side, facing the lake. Momentarily stunned but not unconscious, he knew what the huge splash meant when he heard it. The van was in the water.

A full 30 seconds passed before his senses returned and he could think clearly. From where he lay, he could see the lake and the van resting in the deep water at a strange angle. Through the shock, he could hear voices yelling for help from within the doomed vehicle. He watched as it continued its slow roll over to its side and sank below the surface. The screaming ended.

The last he saw of the van were the tires of the now upside-down vehicle as they disappeared under the water.

Knowing what he needed to do, Evan attempted to stand. He would save his family. Immediately his plan fell apart when his fractured collarbone impeded his ability to get off the ground. Undeterred, he rolled to his stomach, planning to use his good arm to help himself get up. He'd go into the lake, using only one arm if needed.

As he rolled over, he screamed in agony and looked down at his right leg. It lay at a strange angle with the foot facing backward.

Several seconds went by before the pain subsided, and he could breathe again. Collapsing to his side, he looked back to the lake and the van. Unable to help, he wept in dismay as he watched the water for several minutes as air bubbles continued to rise to the surface. The whole time, all he could think about was his family, slowly dying without air, and what it must be like.

Already close to dark, and since the van was under water, no one noticed the injured boy for nine hours. The whole time he lay awake in the same spot staring into the water, crying out his sister's name over and over again.

For more than a decade, that image had remained with him, and his obsession with what it would be like to die that way – slowly and unable to breathe – grew.

In his teens, he'd drowned some small animals. Eventually, while in college, he'd killed some larger animals, but that hadn't satisfied his need. He hoped that sitting back and watching other people suffocate, the way his family had, would give him peace and make his family feel a little closer.

After sitting next to the body of Leon Conway for a full 15 minutes, Evan got up and left the house.

Chapter 15

As a teacher's aide at Central Elementary School, Candice Wallace rotated between the three preschool classrooms and knew most of the kids well. One of her responsibilities was to ensure that all the kids were dismissed correctly, either on a bus or with a designated person to pick them up.

Today, things were winding down, with most of the children gone from the foyer where they gathered for dismissal. She then noticed Ashley Conway standing against the wall, dressed in shorts, a T-shirt with cute baby bears on it, and with her backpack on. This far into the school year, Candice knew which parents were here early and which ones tended to be late, and Ashley was almost always one of the first to go and never one of the last.

Walking to the girl, Candice asked, "Ashley. Did your dad say anything about possibly being a little late today?"

Shaking her head, the young child replied, "No."

"Okay. I'm sure he'll be here soon."

Fifteen minutes later, her dad still hadn't arrived, so Candice led the child back to the school office.

Speaking to the school secretary, she said, "Deb, can you

pull up the phone number for Ashley Conway's father? He's a no-show and this isn't like him."

The secretary provided the info, and Candice called his cell phone, getting voicemail. "Mr. Conway," she began, "this is Candice Wallace at Central Elementary. No one showed up to get your daughter this afternoon. Can you please call the school? Thanks."

She led the child to a padded bench and said, "I'm sure he's on the way. We'll give him a few more minutes."

Twenty minutes later, they called Sandy Conway but, knowing the mother's work schedule, they weren't surprised to find the call going to voicemail.

A few minutes later, Candice placed another call. "Is this Lori Rodriguez?" she asked when the phone was answered.

"Yes, it is."

"This is Candice Wallace at Central Elementary. We have you listed as an emergency contact for Ashley Conway. Is that correct?"

"Yes, I am. Is there a problem? Is she okay?" the woman asked with concern in her voice.

"She's fine, but no one has come to pick her up today, and no one is answering either of the parents' phones. It's almost an hour past dismissal time, and I hoped you could come and get her."

"Absolutely. I'll be there in less than 10 minutes."

Hanging up, Lori Rodriguez glanced at the calendar on the wall. There'd been a few times the Conways had asked her to pick Ashley up from school, but seeing today's date blank, she knew her assistance hadn't been expected today.

She grabbed her purse, headed to the car, and arrived at the school in a few minutes. Familiar with the building from when her own kids attended there nearly 20 years earlier, she headed directly to the school office.

As soon as she entered, she saw her neighbor's sweet

daughter. The child immediately stood and waved. "Hi, Miss Lori!"

"Hey, Ashley. I'm going to take you home."

"Okay," the child answered with her typical huge grin.

"Thanks for coming in," said the woman behind the counter that separated the office staff from the waiting area.

"Her parents ask me to pick her up occasionally, and I didn't have anything going on today, so coming in wasn't a problem," Lori explained.

She pulled her wallet from her purse to show her identification to the woman behind the desk.

"Thanks, Mrs. Rodriguez. You're all set to take her," the secretary said as she finished copying Lori's name into the sign-out log.

Looking back at Ashley, Lori said, "Let's go, kiddo. We'll get you home."

As they walked to the car, Lori asked, "Any idea where your dad is?"

"At home, I guess," the girl answered.

Considering it briefly, she decided that Leon must have gotten tied up with something work-related and lost track of time.

The two chatted briefly on the short trip to Lori's house.

Upon arrival at her home, Lori assisted the child with removing the seatbelt, and they headed across the street to the Conways' house.

Walking to the front door, Lori turned the knob and found it unlocked. As she swung the door open, a thought started to form in her mind. One of caution. Maybe she should go in first and make sure there wasn't a problem before allowing the little girl in.

However, the 50 year-old woman's response wasn't fast enough for an excited child who wanted to see her beloved father.

Bursting past her neighbor, Ashley raced into the house,

oblivious to the call for her to wait. The child knew where her dad would be this time of day and went directly to his home office.

She entered the room running while yelling, "Daddy, where are you?" and then came to an abrupt halt as she found herself standing over the body of her dad, whose face had become purple and grossly deformed.

As Lori closed the front door, she heard the blood-curdling scream come from the child who'd be forever damaged by what she had seen.

Chapter 16

Officer Amanda Visser sat in her patrol car, parked by the entrance to the regional medical center. She was finishing the report regarding a traffic accident she'd recently handled. Minutes before, she completed interviewing the accident victim, who'd been brought here with minor injuries by ambulance.

So far, it had been a quiet day with nothing out of the ordinary going on when her radio sounded.

"Three-six."

"Three-six, go ahead," Amanda answered.

"Respond to 4728 Baxter Place. Possible DOA."

"4728 Baxter Place. Responding from the medical center."

Flipping on her emergency lights, Officer Visser maneuvered away from the hospital. Only as she approached the main road did she engage the siren.

Traffic was light because peak school traffic had finished for the day and most workers hadn't yet started their journeys home. Six minutes later, she pulled up at the address.

"Three-six," Amanda said.

"Go ahead, three-six."

"On scene."

"Ten-four. EMS is three minutes away," the dispatcher said.

"Understood."

Exiting the patrol car, she headed to the house, where she saw a middle-aged woman trying to comfort a hysterical young girl, her face soaked with tears.

"Ma'am. What happened? Is she injured?" Amanda asked.

"No, she isn't hurt, but she saw her father's body before I could stop her. I'm the neighbor, and I brought her home from school. We found him on the floor in the office. Something's terribly wrong!" The distraught woman explained.

"In what way?"

Nodding her head toward the child, the woman shook her head, indicating she wouldn't answer. Instead, she said, "You better see for yourself. Inside and to the right. Last room down the hall."

Officer Visser entered the home and followed the directions to the office. As she stepped into the room, she moved slowly, taking in everything and making sure not to disturb the scene. The first thing she saw were the legs of someone flat on the floor. As she moved further in, the rest of the body became visible. The officer noticed two things at once, the deep purple coloring of the face, which was caused by a lack of oxygen, and the large mass covering the mouth and nose.

Amanda silently cursed and then continued to examine the scene. An expended Taser cartridge lay on the floor with the wires still connected to the victim. Also, there was a toppled coffee cup and a large stain on the carpet. She assumed the stain came from the contents of the coffee cup. Taser AFIDs were all around the man

Taking the radio microphone attached to her shoulder, she took a couple of deep breaths to make sure her voice was free of the emotion she felt.

"Three-six"

"Go ahead, three-six."

"Cancel EMS, DOA. Respond the supervisor, detectives, and crime scene techs here. Will need medical examiner, too."

"Understood," the dispatcher said.

"Stand by for my call."

Not wanting the specifics to be heard by anyone using a radio scanner, especially the media, Amanda took out her cell phone and called into the dispatch center.

"Hey, Amanda. What've you got there?"

"Hey, Conor. It's another spray foam in the throat."

"No way! In a house this time?"

"Yeah, no doubt. This guy has been down for several hours at least."

"All right. I'll get everyone on the way."

Putting her phone away, Amanda Visser took one last look at the crime scene, checking for anything she'd missed before. A strange object on the desk drew her attention. It looked like a small sword sticking through a rock. Probably a novelty paperweight, she thought. Not seeing anything else, she quickly searched the rest of the home, looking for anything else that could be important. She found nothing of interest until she stepped through the utility room and reached the rear door that opened into the backyard. The frame was heavily damaged, and the door sat partially ajar. Using a gloved hand, she pulled the door open, making sure not to touch the knob in case there were fingerprints on it. Once it was open, she examined the entryway and the yard. The door had a partial footprint above the knob, where someone had crudely kicked it in. The yard had a fence on three sides with open access to the front of the house. There was nothing else of interest to be seen.

She retraced her steps through the home until she reached the front entrance and approached the woman who was sitting, holding the still-hysterical child.

"Ma'am, do you know where the child's mother is?" Amanda inquired.

"She's an airline pilot. I don't know her routes, but she's often gone for a couple of days at a time."

"Would you have her cell phone number?"

Lori dug her phone from her pocket and located the address book entry for Sandy Conway. Amanda copied the number into her notepad and would give it to the detectives when they arrived.

"Okay, there's going to be a lot of activity and many people arriving soon. You said you're a neighbor. What's your name and address?" She asked.

"I'm Lori Rodriguez, and I live there," she said, pointing across the street.

When she pointed, Amanda spotted another marked Tucson police vehicle arriving.

"It'll be several hours at least before the house will be available again. Maybe you could take the little girl to your place for a while?"

"That would be good. She doesn't need to see all this commotion," Lori agreed.

"Good. The detectives will be over in a little while to talk to you both. Is there anything from inside that she needs? Medications? Maybe a comforting toy?"

"She isn't on any medications. She's spent the night at my house before, so I know that."

Lori tried to ask Ashley if she wanted anything from her room, but the child didn't seem to hear her – her crying was too intense.

"Is that her school bag?" the officer asked.

"Yes."

"Let me see it."

As Amanda took the bag, she noticed that her supervisor, Sergeant Gary Billings, had arrived and was standing behind her.

"You okay with this, Sarge?" she asked, unsure how much of the conversation the sergeant had heard.

"You aren't getting stuff out of the room where this happened. Right?"

"Of course not."

"Yeah, then go ahead."

"I'll be right back," Amanda told the woman.

She went back into the house, her shift sergeant following.

"It's the last room down the hall. I only went a couple of steps into the room," she explained.

As she stepped into the child's bedroom, Sergeant Billings went past her to see the crime scene for himself.

In the child's room, everything looked as expected. The bed was unmade, with a pillow, clothes, and stuffed animals on it. Toys lay scattered about the room, and the dresser had two drawers partly open. There were several drawings on the wall. They were drawn by a child but with much more skill than Amanda would expect. The child had some artistic talent.

Walking to the bed, she opened the backpack and dumped the contents. There were several folders, some wrinkled papers, and a lunchbox.

On the bed, close to the pillow, lay a light green stuffed hippo wearing a purple bow around its neck. She took it and placed it in the bag. A thick storybook lay on the stand beside the bed, and Amanda added that. At the foot of the bed, she found a pair of pajamas, which she stuffed in next to the hippo.

Taking the backpack and lunchbox, she headed to the kitchen. She deposited the lunchbox on the counter and started opening cabinets looking for the kind of treats only a child would eat, and found a box of chewy fruit snacks. She dropped several packs in the backpack and turned to leave, seeing Sergeant Billings approaching.

"This guy changed from darts to a Taser? That's odd," he said.

"According to the updates we got, the darts weren't working as he planned," Amanda said.

"True. Still, it's interesting."

"More like disturbing," Amanda commented.

They left the house and saw two additional patrol cars arriving. Lori was holding Ashley as the child clung to her neck, still sobbing. Amanda Visser handed the bag to a fellow officer and quietly asked him to escort Lori home.

"Visser," Sergeant Billings said, "no one else goes in until the detectives or the crime scene unit arrives, and they say it's clear. You stay here. I'll work with the others responding to start knocking on doors and asking if anyone saw anything."

Chapter 17

MACKENZIE BELL SAT ON A BLANKET IN THE PARK, ENJOYING time with her family. Her three sons, all elementary-school age, were on a playset jumping around and being silly. She dug into the blue, long-handled cooler, getting out the food for their late-afternoon picnic.

Her husband, Kevin, sat with her, keeping his attention on their children. Both of them treasured their family time.

Kevin worked in the 911 call center as a dispatcher, so it was uncommon for them to have time like this, as they both had irregular and often conflicting work schedules. Therefore, this time in the park, after school as a family, was a special event.

An audible tone sounded from Mac's cell phone. The couple both recognized the sound that all work-related calls made.

"Are you on call this week?" Kevin asked.

"No."

Taking out the phone, she already had a suspicion as to the situation. "Bell," she said.

"Hey, Mac. It's Conor in dispatch. Sorry to interrupt your day off, but we've had another spray foam killing."

"What's the status?"

"The scene is secured. One DOA. Crime Scene techs are en route, and I left a message for your partner, but he hasn't called in yet."

"Okay. Send me the address, and I'll be on my way."

She disconnected the call and gave Kevin an apologetic smile.

"Let me guess, It's related to something designated a major case, and you're the assigned detective, so a day off doesn't matter."

Nodding, she added, "Yeah. Spray-foam guy again. Sorry."

Returning the smile, Kevin answered, "I know how it works. The kids and I'll get a rideshare home." The disappointment was evident in his voice.

Mac reached into the cooler and grabbed the sandwich she'd made before leaving the house, with the word "Mom" written on the zipped bag.

They both stood and shared a quick kiss before Mac headed to the car, and Kevin went to the kids to tell them their mom had to leave and that it was time to come and eat.

As Mac got to the car, she hit the button on her keychain, and the trunk opened. Her fingerprint opened the small lockbox securely mounted to the car's frame. From inside, she removed her department-issued Glock19 in its holster and her credentials. She hung her badge from a lanyard around her neck. The holstered gun she clipped to her right hip.

After getting in, she linked her phone to the vehicle's navigation system and tapped the address texted over from dispatch. The console in the dashboard immediately displayed a map and directions on how to get to the unfamiliar address.

Being on the other side of town, it took almost 15 minutes for her to arrive, more than enough time to eat the sandwich. As she pulled up to the scene, driving her personal car, a uniformed officer tried to wave her to pass on through, but she ignored him, stopping alongside the curb, one house away.

As she stepped out of the car, the officer approached, she assumed to tell her to move. Then he saw the lanyard. Mac chuckled at his reaction when he cleanly shifted mental gears and said, "Hey, Detective. They're waiting for you at the house."

Mac smiled at him. "Thanks."

Approaching the house, she recognized Sergeant Billings. "Afternoon, Detective," he said in greeting.

"Hey, Sarge."

"Do you know Officer Amanda Visser?"

"Yeah, I've worked with her a couple of times."

"Good. She was the first to arrive and is up by the front of the house. She can give you the best account of what happened, but your guy switched from darts to a Taser," Billings explained.

Confused by the change, Mac asked, "Are we sure it's the same guy?"

"I wasn't at the first scene, but I saw the photos, and this has the same foam in the mouth and nose."

"Okay, thanks. Any ETA on the crime-scene team?"

"Should be here any minute."

"Great," Mac responded.

She continued to the house and recognized Amanda Visser standing outside by the front door. "Officer Visser."

"Hey, Detective."

"I hear you were the first one here."

"I drew the short straw, I guess."

"I also understand you sent the witnesses to a house across the street?"

"The victim's five-year-old daughter found him. She's a wreck. She didn't need to see all of us here too. I know letting them leave the scene isn't protocol, but I felt it was necessary."

With a questioning look, Mac replied, "Necessary, no. But

it was the right decision. Let me know if anyone questions you about it."

Officer Visser nodded, glad not to have irritated the detective.

"I heard a rumor that you recently took the detective exam," Mac said.

"I did. But I haven't heard the results yet; it should be any day now."

"Well, I hope you get it. Let's pretend you did. Walk me through the house. What did you think, feel, and suspect when you first went inside?" Mac instructed.

Entering the residence, Amanda nervously began recalling her initial impressions, wanting to sound competent. "At first, things seemed normal. No strange sounds. Everything was still. Then I started down the hall and could smell the death. You know what I mean. The victim's bowels had released, and there were other smells. Those of a dead body after a few hours."

Mac nodded her head, knowing exactly what the officer meant.

The two approached the office door, and Mac had the officer explain, in detail, everything she saw. Then the two entered the large 20-by-20 room, staying well clear of the body and making sure not to disturb any evidence.

Reaching the other side of the room, they stood on the far side of the desk, and Mac said, "Impressions?"

"He was Tased when entering the room. So the attacker was waiting in here."

"Why do you say that?" Mac asked.

"The feet. They're closer to the door. When a body contracts from a Taser, it crumples forward, and the victim's head is closer to the desk," Amanda explained.

"Good. Tell me more."

"He's about 10 feet into the room, so the assailant wasn't standing out in the open. If he had been, Mr. Conway would have stopped by the doorway, not so far into the room."

Mac could hear Officer Visser's confidence growing the more she spoke.

"So where was he hiding?"

Amanda looked around the room and said, "The closet's the only place where no one would see him."

"Okay. So there's good reason to believe the attacker spent time in the closet. Why does that matter?" Mac asked.

"We want to make sure the crime-scene techs swab it all down for trace evidence."

"Exactly," the detective said. "What else do you see?"

"I'm not seeing anything else."

"Are you sure there isn't anything else in here that caught your attention? I think there is. It caught mine."

After a few seconds, Amanda gave Mac a curious look.

Mac pointed at the desk and said, "Look at the desk. Does anything catch your eye?"

"The weird paperweight. I noticed it when I first entered the room."

"Exactly. The whole time we've been in here, I've wanted to check it out. It stands out and is intriguing. I bet most visitors to this room ask about it."

"Probably. So?"

"A detective needs to try and think like the perpetrator. We know he was in here for a period of time, waiting for Mr. Conway. If you were alone in this room waiting, what's the first thing you'd do?"

"I'd check out that thing on the desk."

Mac nodded. "Exactly. I'd almost guarantee our subject touched it."

Chapter 18

THE FOLLOWING MORNING, THE TWO DETECTIVES GATHERED with their supervisor once more to review the case. As Mac walked into the conference room, she saw her partner seated at the table. "It's nice of you to join us today," she said drily.

From his seat at the table, Dan explained, "I was with the kids at the aquatic center. I put my phone in a locker while I swam. By the time I saw the message and called in, the scene had been cleared."

Not done teasing, Mac said, "You must have been in the water a long time. We were on the scene for over six hours."

Lieutenant Miller, knowing the call had only lasted three hours, smiled. He appreciated his people and seeing their good relationship pleased him.

"Okay, you two, battle this out later. Mac, thanks for being available yesterday. Tell us what's new."

Mac started her presentation. "There are many things. The two most important are, first, yesterday's victim was alive when asphyxiated by the foam. We found obvious signs on the body. I believe this was what the assailant had been after all along and he finally achieved it. The second most important thing was the complete change in his pattern of attack. This time, the attack happened in a home, not on a secluded path, and he changed away from the dart guns. I think he learned the drugs weren't as manageable as he hoped, so he switched his method of incapacitating his victims."

The lieutenant agreed and said, "This means he's evolving and adapting as needed. He's becoming more dangerous as time goes on."

"True, but what's his goal? Have we seen it?" Dan asked.

Mac added her opinion. "If a killer strangles someone, they're basically wrestling the person to death. By using the foam, our killer can apply it and then sit back and watch his victim die. I think that's what he wants. The ability to take in the moment of death."

"I don't disagree, but there are simpler ways to do the same thing. Like a zip-tie around the neck," Dan said.

"Therefore, there's something special about the foam insulation," Mac stated.

Miller thought a minute and added, "You're mixing two types of deaths. Your example of a zip tie would be strangulation. The foam is more like a controlled drowning, similar to water filling the lungs. That might be what he needs; a specific type of death."

The others were silent after hearing their boss's idea, with neither of the detectives having a better idea.

Eventually, Lieutenant Miller spoke again. "Did you learn anything else from the scene?" he asked.

"Several things. Many complete sets of footprints were in the dirt at the previously failed attempt along the path. We weren't sure which belonged to the attacker. We found a partial boot print at the house yesterday on the door he kicked in. It wasn't enough to get the size, but we could compare the tread pattern to the ones at the previous scene and now know which footprints were his and that he wears a size-10 boot. By itself, this isn't super valuable, but when you add it to the other things we know from the blood and DNA, we're starting to get a clearer picture of what he looks like.

"There were a couple of things that didn't go our way. Officers talked to every homeowner within a quarter-mile of the Conway residence, and no one remembers anything. A couple of people thought they might have seen a guy walking, but they weren't confident that it wasn't someone from the neighborhood.

"Also, we tracked the serial number on the Taser cartridge, and it came back to a shipment stolen from a police supply company in Tennessee six months ago. In the robbery, six Tasers and 50 cartridges were taken. AFIDs and cartridges with those serial numbers have been found in Miami, Boston, Toronto, and Houston. So it looks like the Taser serial numbers won't do us any good.

"On a positive note, we'll soon know the brand of rubber gloves he uses. At the scene, we found a decorative paper-weight with a mini sword sticking out of a stone. It had a sharp point on it, and the crime lab found a rubber glove fragment where he handled it, and it ripped a piece off the glove. They're analyzing it now."

"Have you started putting together a preliminary profile?" The lieutenant asked.

Dan spoke up, "From the DNA sample we recovered at his second attack, we know we're looking for a white male with brown hair and blue eyes. He stands about six feet tall and has O-positive blood. Now we can add that he wears a size 10 shoe. That's all we know. Beyond that, he's adapting and changing, which indicates he's younger, probably in his twenties."

Mac added, "He seems to attack mostly in the mornings, suggesting he's a second or third-shift worker, if he's employed. Also, his behavior when he confronted the two girls in the county park suggests he has a strong connection with kids. Maybe he's a father, or the girls reminded him of a specific child he has a connection to."

"I'd like to take our information and your profile and send it to the FBI. Let their profilers look and see if there's anything we aren't seeing," Lieutenant Miller said.

"Lieutenant, please don't! We can handle this. We don't need the feds coming in and taking over," Dan insisted.

"I'm not talking about bringing them in. They can collaborate with us remotely, firm up the profile and make suggestions. The investigation is yours. I don't plan to ask them to come here, not yet, anyway. But remember, if any evidence shows this guy has operated in other states, it automatically becomes their investigation."

The expression on Dan's face made his reluctance to ask for outside input clear. He glanced at his partner, who nodded.

"Alright, as long as they're just collaborating remotely and not showing up here," Dan clarified.

Chapter 19

VALORIE LEE WAS AN ASIAN AMERICAN WOMAN WHO WORKED in human resources at a local manufacturing company. Divorced and in her late thirties, she lived alone with her cat Wilbur in a two-bedroom condo.

Today, being Sunday, she had the day off and was returning home from meeting friends for breakfast, followed by a trip to the grocery store.

Approaching her home, she pressed the button on her car's visor, and the garage door slowly started opening. It had fully opened by the time Valorie got there and pulled in, and she immediately closed the door. She was always security-conscious but a story she'd recently read online about someone being attacked in his home had her taking no chances.

Before getting out of the vehicle, the garage door closed and the back hatch of her Toyota SUV was opening.

There were three bags in the car, and Valorie grabbed the first two and headed into the house. Moving through the entry hall, she passed the living room and entered the dining room. To the left was the kitchen, and to the right was her bedroom. As Valorie approached the table, she paused. Something felt wrong, but she didn't know what. Listening, she could hear only the central air conditioner. She sniffed and didn't smell anything. The woman focused for a couple more seconds, but nothing specific registered. She'd been up late the night before watching a movie about a woman who'd been murdered and figured, coupled with the recent news story, the strange feeling was all in her head.

Dismissing the warning, Valorie set the bags down on the dining room table and turned to get the remaining groceries from her car.

As she did, someone stepped from the living room and blocked her path back to the garage.

It was a man in his early to mid-twenties who stood about six feet tall. He looked a bit disheveled but not dirty, and he wore an old green ball cap on his head. His expression remained neutral. He held a spray can in his gloved left hand, and in his right was a Taser, which he brought up and pointed at her.

Already on alert, Valorie spun to her left, turning to flee when she felt a single sharp stabbing pain in her left side.

The Taser barb passed through her blouse and embedded itself between her beltline and lowest rib.

Valorie would never know if it was her petite size or speed that caused the second barb to miss. It landed harmlessly on the floor and thereby failed to complete the circuit needed to deliver the intended electrical shock.

Not understanding this or that the weapon had a second cartridge that her assailant was preparing to fire, she charged the four feet into her bedroom. She slammed the door depressing the lock in the knob. As the door slammed shut, it caught on the wire and ripped the Taser barb from her side.

Yelping in pain, Valorie touched her side, and her finger came back with a tiny smear of blood that the needle-sized barb had made.

Almost immediately, the assailant started pounding on the door and screaming curses.

Reaching into her pocket, she pulled out her phone and dialed 911. Looking at the screen, she saw that the call failed because there was no service. This didn't make sense to her because a cell tower was visible from her backyard.

The door shuddered, impacted by a foot or shoulder from the other side. Her resolve set, Valorie dived across the bed, reached into the nightstand and withdrew her purple Sig Sauer P238 semi-automatic pistol. Still lying across the bed, she chambered a round and fired through the center of the door just after another blow made a visible crack in the frame.

For a full 30 seconds, she lay across the bed, pointing her gun at the bedroom door, ready to fire again if anyone touched it. With her hearing impaired by the loud gunshot, Valorie didn't know if the assailant was still outside the door.

Eventually, she approached and turned the knob, wondering how she'd react if there were a body on the ground.

Valorie yanked the door open with the Sig up and her finger on the trigger. There was no one there, but a good amount of blood splatter covered a section of the floor. She'd hit him.

A sudden movement startled her as Wilbur raced past her heading away from the commotion. Feeling relieved that the cat was safe, she looked at her phone again and saw there was now full service. Slowly and with her heart racing, Valorie exited the room, her foot almost hitting the red spray can lying on the floor.

As she walked, her eyes took in the microwave on the counter with the glass door shattered from her bullet that had passed through her attacker.

The traumatized woman followed the blood trail out of the house while dialing 911 again. The blood drops were spaced every few inches, and she wondered if she would stumble upon the man collapsed on the ground.

By the time she got to the driveway and the 911 operator answered, approaching sirens could be heard.

Several of her neighbors, having heard the shot, had called the police and were now coming outside to see what was happening. She hung up the call, knowing that help was already coming.

Understanding the man had fled, she flipped the safety on the pistol and tucked it in the back of her pants, the barrel still noticeably warm for the shot she'd fired.

She pulled her shirt over it. She'd gladly hand the weapon over to the police but figured everything would go better if she weren't standing in the road holding a gun when they arrived.

Chapter 20

DETECTIVE DAN FELTY SPED ACROSS TOWN. AS HE DID, HE glanced over at his silent partner, noting the expression of failure on her face. They were heading to the fourth home invasion and Taser attack in the last two weeks.

Ever since the attack and murder at the Conway residence, the killer had been busy, striking in a similar way every two to four days. So far, he'd proven to be quite efficient. In each case, they found a single foamed victim without any new evidence. If there wasn't a break in the case soon, their lieutenant would ask the FBI to step in. And as much as Dan didn't want that, he understood.

All they knew about this call was that there was another Taser attack in a private residence, and the victim had survived.

Mac worked on the vehicle-mounted computer as Dan drove. She checked the dispatch information. "We were told this was a Taser attack, but the initial call to dispatch came in for a gunshot," she read. "The first officer on the scene canceled the ambulance and requested other units to look for the attacker."

"A survivor? Hopefully, this'll be the break in the case we need," Dan commented.

Several minutes later, they arrived on the scene and were met by a uniformed officer who approached, carrying a clear, sealed evidence bag.

"Hey, Detectives."

"Morning. What's up?" Mac asked.

"I was first on the scene. The victim is up by the house.

"Your guy waited for her in the house until she came inside with her groceries. He appeared in the kitchen, between her and the garage. Fortunately, the bedroom where she kept her gun was only a few steps away, and she managed to lock herself inside. When he tried to break down the door, she fired through the door, and he fled.

"When I arrived, the suspect had already gone. I took a quick drive around the block but didn't see anything. There's a faint blood trail, but he isn't losing enough to follow it easily. I called for the dog, but his handler is tied up on another call. Dispatch is trying to get the sheriff's department to bring theirs over."

As he filled them in, he handed over the clear evidence bag. Inside they saw a semi-automatic pistol. "She says she only fired once. The gun can hold seven rounds, and there's a single round missing from the magazine."

Mac looked at it. "It's purple!" she said with a hint of glee in her voice.

"Well, that's special," Dan commented.

"I like it. I want a purple gun. Do you think the department would let me have one?" Mac asked jokingly. She kept her voice low so no one else would hear the conversation.

"If they do, you'll need a new partner. No one would take a purple gun seriously."

"It might look kinda silly, but it worked well for her today. It probably saved her life," the officer said.

Unable to dispute the fact, Dan headed toward the house.

"Let's take a quick look inside before the evidence techs arrive. I don't want to be in their way."

Drops of blood stood out clearly on the white linoleum floor. Careful not to step on any, they went inside to check out the scene. Several things jumped out at them. One was the used Taser cartridge, and even better was the can of spray foam on the floor with the name FoamX in big letters. This was the first can they'd recovered.

"Well, this is promising," Mac said as she bent down and, without touching anything, snapped a picture with her phone of the bottom of the can and the lot number clearly stamped there.

While she investigated the can, Dan went to the bedroom door and looked at the bullet hole. It was lower than he would have expected, but he stood next to it and saw it lined up with the middle of his abdomen. Dan thought that the suspect stood about his height. So he had a good idea where on the body the would-be killer had been wounded, though the bullet might have struck an arm or hand.

As the two detectives were conferring, the officer called to them, "Hey, Detectives. The crime-scene guys are here."

Not wanting to be in the way, Dan and Mac left the house and found the homeowner sitting in the front seat of a police cruiser with the door open.

"Ma'am, we're detectives Felty and Bell. Can you tell us what happened here today?"

The detectives listened for the next 15 minutes and asked questions, getting the whole story about what the woman had seen and experienced.

At the end of the interview, Mac asked a last question, "Did you get a good look at his face? Do you think you could identify him?"

"For a moment, we stared right at one another. I know exactly what he looks like."

Chapter 21

DAN AND MAC LOOKED AT ONE ANOTHER, THRILLED TO HAVE A survivor who knew what the attacker looked like.

Dan asked, "Ma'am, do you think you could come downtown and work with one of the artists to get a composite sketch of the man who attacked you? It would be extremely helpful."

"I saw him and could recognize him or his picture, but I'm not sure I could describe him well enough to have someone draw him."

"Our experts are excellent, and their software does a great job. They'll work with you to pull it together," Mac explained.

"When would I have to go in?" Valorie asked.

"Normally, we'd want you to go in immediately, but being a Sunday, the artist isn't in. I'll set something up for first thing tomorrow. Will that work?" Dan asked.

"I can do that. Where do I need to go?"

As they spoke, an SUV from the sheriff's department pulled in. The deputy got out, and Mac approached. "I'm Mackenzie, one of the detectives on the case, but everyone calls me Mac. My partner is Dan."

Shaking her hand, the deputy said, "I'm Bobby. Rex is in the car. I understand you want to track someone?"

"Our subject assaulted a woman in the house. She shot and wounded the assailant, and he fled," Mac explained.

Understanding what he needed to do, the deputy opened the back of the vehicle, and a Belgian Malinois jumped out. The large dog was golden tan with a dark face and wore a black bulletproof vest that covered most of its torso and had the words 'Sheriff's K9' in white letters on the side.

Mac led the pair into the house, where blood stained the floor. The canine sniffed the area and then headed back outside to where more blood was on the sidewalk. Again the dog investigated, and the deputy spoke to the animal in a language unfamiliar to Mac, then the trio headed down the sidewalk.

After walking for about a quarter mile and making several turns, Rex stopped along a residential street. The dog and handler worked for several minutes but could no longer pick up a scent.

Rex stopped sniffing, walked to his handler, and sat at his side.

"When he does that, it means the scent's gone. I suspect the attacker parked his car here," the deputy explained.

Understanding the situation, Mac requested officers to knock on doors to see if anyone remembered seeing a car or truck there in the morning.

While they were at the scene, Lieutenant Miller had texted the detectives saying their presence was required for a meeting at 2 pm, so they headed back to their car.

They had enough time before the meeting to grab a late lunch from a sandwich shop they were both fond of.

Dan and Mac entered the restaurant and, being after the noon rush, were able to order immediately. Taking their food to a seat where no one would overhear them, Dan asked, "What are you thinking?"

Mac picked up the wrap she had ordered and, before biting into it, said, "The sketch may break the investigation wide open. But I'm almost as interested in tracing the lot number on the foam can. That could lead us to who purchased it."

"True," Dan agreed. "I already had dispatch contact the area hospitals and have them watching for a gunshot wound."

Continuing to eat, the detectives discussed the case until the time came to leave for their meeting.

As they entered the station, Lieutenant Miller met them. "Good timing, guys. We've got a video call with the FBI in a few minutes."

The three of them walked together to the conference room.

"Why are we meeting with them?" Dan asked.

"They want to review the profile we sent them."

"We sent the information to them almost two weeks ago. I'd assumed we would've heard much sooner," Mac said.

"I guess they're busy," Miller commented.

Mac found the link for the call in her email, selected it, and saw the blue emblem for the FBI appear on the large screen. Ten seconds later, a man's face appeared. He was Caucasian with a mustache and a friendly expression.

"Good afternoon. I'm Special Agent Ben Fox. I'm a profiler with the FBI," said the Virginia-based agent.

The three Tucson police officers identified themselves. Then Lieutenant Miller asked, "Have you had a chance to review the profile we sent over?"

"Yes, but can you first update me on the status of your investigation? Anything new could impact our findings."

For several minutes Dan spoke, passing along all the new information, especially what had happened earlier that day.

When he finished, Agent Fox nodded, contemplating the news, then said, "Our team discussed this and did some research. You have a good foundation, and we agree with your assessment. The way your guy is killing is very interesting. The switching from drugs to Taser is a significant change in MO, suggesting neither method is important to him. The foam killing is what matters.

"His victims have been old and young, male and female, black, white, and Asian, so he isn't targeting a specific demographic. Also, he's task-focused and isn't lashing out in anger at his victims. They're simply a means to his end, which seems to be the foam."

Dan half-raised his hands while looking at his colleagues, indicating that what he was hearing wasn't new information.

The agent continued, "What we came up with that you didn't have documented is these are what we call two-phased attacks. First, incapacitate and then kill. This is far more complex than just shooting someone and explains why he has had multiple unsuccessful runs.

"His ability to plan his attacks is much stronger than his ability to execute them. He probably has carried out simpler attacks in the past before building up to these more complex acts. Based on this and the other information, we suspect he isn't physically imposing and is probably a loner. He may well live alone or has a private place where he knows he can plan and store the drugs, Tasers, and dart guns. Does all that make sense?"

All three Tucson officers nodded, unsure of the new information's value.

"I know that wasn't very beneficial, but you wanted us to validate your profile, so I covered it first. There is something that might be a bit more interesting," the agent said.

"What's that?" Mac asked.

"Back in 2016, we began tracking animal cruelty in the National Incident-Based Reporting System. That's the same system used to track all other violent crimes in the country. We already have a load of data on animal abuse cases. When your case came up, we searched and found something you might find interesting. As you know, serial killers often perfect their craft on animals. Usually stolen pets."

"We looked into that initially and didn't find anything. Also, the foam nozzle is too large to work well on a dog or cat. Certainly nothing smaller," Dan explained.

"I understand, but you searched within the state of Arizona. These images may be a bit disturbing," Fox said.

The agent clicked a few keys, and his image on the screen vanished, and a picture of a dead cow appeared.

The animal was lying on its side in a grassy field, its eyes bulging outward, and its throat was grossly enlarged. The familiar sight of insulating foam protruding from the mouth and nose startled the detectives.

The three Tucson officers were silent as they stared at the image. Then suddenly, the picture on the screen changed again, and they were looking at a close-up shot of the head of a second cow. The animal's markings were different, making it clear they weren't looking at the same cow, but the atrocity was identical.

Special Agent Fox continued, "These cows were found with short chains around their necks and attached to nearby trees. Presumably to keep them from getting away during the assault."

Overcoming his shock, Dan replied, "We looked for similar issues and didn't find these. When and where did this happen?"

"You didn't find it because it happened almost two years ago in Montana."

After a moment to consider the new information Mac asked, "Were there only the two cases?"

"Two cows on the same ranch on the same weekend," the FBI profiler said.

"Did they use a dart gun or Taser to control the animals?" Lieutenant Miller asked.

Shaking his head, Agent Fox said, "No. Nothing like that.

The investigating sheriff thinks they were hooked up with the chain like a leash and led to the tree where they were secured."

"Can you give us the sheriff's and ranch owner's names? I want to call them since there are human victims. They might have a different perspective," Dan said.

"I'll send it over," Agent Fox agreed.

Lieutenant Miller added, "The new information needs to be added to the profile. Most people wouldn't walk up to a twelve-hundred-pound cow and leash it. Our guy feels comfortable around large animals."

"That's quite true and important in light of this new data," the agent agreed.

"So, from what you've heard, do you have any recommendations?" Mac asked.

"Actually, we do. When you consider his initial failures and today's, the killer has only a 50 percent success rate on his attacks. When he makes mistakes, you learn a little more each time. Such as today. You've gotten several good leads from this last attempt.

"Right now, he's operating and staging attacks as he pleases. It would help if you could get in his head, throw him off his game, and force him to make mistakes. He'll eventually screw up, and that'll lead you to him," Agent Fox explained.

"We could hold a press conference and push his buttons. We've been considering doing that already," Mac said.

The agent nodded. "That's often an effective tool."

Mac looked around the room to see if anyone had additional questions. When no one indicated any, she said, "Thank you for your time today. Can we contact you if there are questions or if new evidence emerges?"

"Absolutely. We will keep this file open. Good luck, detectives; you sure have an unusual case here."

Mac disconnected the call.

Chapter 22

Evan drove with one hand on the wheel as the tears of despair ran down his cheeks. The other hand was clamped tightly on his left side, unsuccessfully trying to stop blood flow.

The bullet had come through the bedroom door and creased his left side. He knew no vital organs had been hit, but a sizeable bloody gash had been opened on the side of his abdomen.

If the bullet had come out the door an inch to the right, it would've missed him, and if it had been an inch to the left, he'd be in critical condition or dead.

Knowing this didn't suppress his fury at his failure. His typical pounding of the steering wheel when enraged wasn't possible as he fought to keep pressure on the wound as he drove.

Arriving at his home, he opened the car door and tried to ignore the increasing pain as he got out of the vehicle. As he shut the door, he was further angered at how much blood had spilled on to the car's cloth seat and how much work it would take to clean it up.

Heading into the house, his self-disgust took another leap as he thought about the can of FoamX he'd left behind. That had been sloppy, and he hated himself for doing something so foolish. Fortunately, he hadn't also dropped the Taser when he was shot.

He walked to the bathroom and looked in the full-length mirror on the door. Removing his shirt, he examined the wound. It was about five inches long and went through the skin, fat, and muscle. Examining the wound track, he could feel that wood fragments from the door had been blasted into him with the bullet.

Evan got a wash rag and a tube of super glue and cleaned the wound as best he could with soap and water, trying to remove the wood fragments as he did. He then spent five minutes trying to hold the gash shut so he could glue it closed. With the injury to his side, he couldn't reach it easily while trying to work by using the mirror. To make it worse, the blood was still flowing steadily, which made the skin too slippery to hold, and he soon realized that this plan was also a failure.

For a full minute, he stood, staring into the mirror at the wound and thinking. Evan knew he couldn't go to a hospital, but he needed help.

Finally, he came to a decision and went to the closet and gathered half a dozen gauze pads and a roll of duct tape.

Ignoring the pain, he filled the wound as best he could with the gauze and then covered it with several duct tape strips. The tape would hurt when he had to remove it, but it should keep the blood trapped inside and off his shirt.

Taking the washcloth, he cleaned the remaining blood off his body and hands and put on a clean shirt.

As he walked to the car, he tossed the bloody shirt with the bullet hole in the overflowing outside trash can. He reminded himself that he needed to have it emptied this week. It had been a while since he'd remembered to walk the trash bin to the street.

Opening the door, he dropped inside, oblivious to the blood on the seat that he sat in.

As he drove, he thought about what had happened and remained furious over his failure with the woman. Everything had proceeded perfectly with the attack until the woman turned towards him. He'd hesitated a moment before firing the Taser. The hesitation wasn't out of doubt or weakness but because he wanted to take in what she looked like alive so he could preserve the memory along with the one of her death.

The pause had allowed her to turn, causing one of the Taser barbs to miss her. This had been a surprise and kept him from reacting fast enough to fire the second Taser cartridge. Because of his error, she'd been able to lock herself in the bedroom.

It took a little over an hour to reach his destination, a small house south of Florence, Arizona, and he repeated his failure over and over again in his mind for the entire trip.

Evan had been here only once before but remembered the directions.

He got out of the car, went to the house, and knocked on the door, but there was no answer.

The pain in his side burned as if on fire, and Evan knew his wound was still bleeding under the layers of tape. This plan needed to work.

Chapter 23

Diego Garcia headed home from the animal clinic feeling a little sad. He was the on-call veterinarian for the clinic this weekend. He had to go in today and put down Mandy, an extremely friendly collie he'd known since joining the practice a little over a year ago.

He knew the elderly dog was in lots of pain, and this had been the right thing to do, but it was still sad. Especially after seeing the seven and ten-year-old boys weeping as they and their mom said their final goodbyes to their beloved friend.

Turning the truck into his driveway, his brow furrowed when he saw a silver sedan parked in front of the house. Pulling in behind it, he stopped and got out. As he approached his home, he saw someone seated on the front porch. It was Evan.

The sadness he was feeling turned to irritation. After what had happened at school, he'd thought he was done dealing with the strange guy. But he kept reappearing.

Almost two weeks before, Diego had begrudgingly called his cousin and arranged an introduction for Evan, who was looking to acquire a Taser.

He thought he'd been clear that, after that favor, he didn't want to hear from Evan again. But here he was.

Evan stood and approached.

Diego could see that there was something wrong. Evan was moving awkwardly and had his hand holding his side. Then he noticed the blood on the other man's pants.

"Hi, Diego. I need your help."

"I told you after the last favor that we're done. I didn't want to hear from you again," Diego said.

"I know, and I'm sorry, but I got hurt and need your help."

"Go to a hospital."

"I can't do that. That's why I'm here," Evan explained.

Diego paused and exhaled deeply. "What did you do? Wait! Don't tell me. I don't want to know. Please go away, Evan."

Evan glared at his only friend. "I know about your past with the gangs. I know the kind of things you were involved in. Still, somehow, you managed to pass a background check and become licensed by the DEA to prescribe schedule-two drugs to your veterinary patients. I could make one call, and they might take your veterinary license."

Diego was furious. He'd spent years breaking from his past and the mistakes he'd made in his youth. Now someone he once considered a friend was threatening to ruin it. However, as angry as he was, he felt one even stronger emotion – fear.

Diego glared at Evan, not sure what to do.

"Look, I'm not here for pain meds. Just some stitches," Evan said, trying to de-escalate the situation. "I tried to seal it up myself, but I can't."

Resigned, Diego said, "If I do this, I don't want to see or hear from you ever again. We aren't friends any longer."

"I promise. This is the last favor I'll ever ask for."

"Get in your car and follow me to the clinic. You aren't getting in my truck with all that blood on your pants."

"Fine, fine. Whatever you want," the killer said.

As Diego led Evan to the clinic, he struggled with what to do. It was illegal to treat a gunshot wound and not report it. Evan hadn't said that he'd been shot, but what other reason could there be why he couldn't go to a hospital? Diego considered calling 911 and having the police meet them at the clinic, but he'd put Evan in touch with his cousin, and he had no idea what the two of them had done. Whatever it was, Diego couldn't have it come back on him. He'd worked too hard to lose it all now.

They arrived 10 minutes later, and Diego pulled around to the rear parking area and out of sight.

They entered through the employee door and made their way to a procedure room.

"Wait here and take off your shirt. I need to get some supplies," Diego said.

He left the room and returned several minutes later.

Motioning to the four-foot-long exam table, he said, "Get up there and lie on your good side."

"How am I supposed to do that? The table is so small," Evan objected.

"We work on animals here, Evan, not people. That's what we have. Get on the table or leave. I'm not doing this on the floor."

Evan complied and was soon on the table with his head and legs hanging off uncomfortably. Diego smiled, thinking of the surgical room down the hall that he could have used, and which had a much larger table.

Returning to his patient, Diego examined the duct tape. Almost no blood had escaped the crude bandaging. He slipped on a pair of latex gloves and plugged the cautery pen into the outlet.

Diego considered warning Evan about what he was about to do but decided against it and forcefully ripped the silver tape off the wound. Evan shrieked, and Diego smiled.

"You could've warned me!" Evan objected.

"Sorry," Diego replied, smiling again.

The bleeding resumed when the veterinarian pulled the gauze out of the wound.

"I think there are some wood fragments in there. I tried to get them out," Evan explained.

Diego didn't say anything but examined the injury, deciding on his approach.

Taking a 10cc syringe with a needle, he stuck the needle into the rubber stopper on a vial of two percent lidocaine. Pulling back on the plunger, he withdrew the medication from the vial.

"I'm going to numb this up, but you'll feel me inject you."

For a wound this size, Diego would typically inject the anesthetic in about 10 locations, five on either side of the wound, to make it numb so the suturing would be bearable. Today he did half as many.

Typically the lidocaine would need about five minutes to take effect, but Diego didn't wait.

Taking a clean square of gauze, he blotted the inside of the wound, looking for where the bleeding was coming from, and found two small blood vessels that were making most of the mess.

"Now, you need to hold still."

Using the cautery pen, he touched the tip, which was heated to more than 2,000 degrees, to each and was rewarded with a sizzling sound and a wisp of smoke.

Evan screamed but didn't move.

Most of the bleeding stopped immediately, and Diego blotted the wound again. He could now see the wood fragments that Evan had mentioned.

Using a pair of forceps, he pulled out the six most obvious ones, not bothering to look more carefully for others.

"Okay, Evan, I got the wood fragments out, and the bleeding is almost stopped."

"Good."

Taking a syringe of sterile saline, the vet squirted it in the wound track to flush away any contaminants. Next, he squirted disinfectant on a gauze pad and cleaned all around the incision.

"I'm going to start suturing. Don't move."

Evan didn't answer.

After Diego had started, Evan said, "That really hurts. Can you numb it up more?"

"Sorry, but I already injected quite a bit. I don't think it's a good idea to use any more."

Evan stayed silent as his rage built. He needed Diego, but he knew his former friend was making this more miserable than necessary.

Diego continued suturing Evan's injury for several minutes before finishing.

"Before I bandage it, do you want to see the sutures?" Diego asked.

"Yes. I want to see what you did. You sure didn't wait for the lidocaine to take effect," the contempt was apparent in Evan's voice.

"I thought I did. I hope it wasn't too painful," Diego replied, barely suppressing his grin.

He handed Evan the mirror, and the killer examined the vet's work.

"Those stitches aren't very close together. There should be more."

"I'm the one who does this all the time. There are enough. As long as you take it easy and don't do anything to pull it open, the wound will hold just fine."

Evan glared at his former friend, not saying anything.

After taping a gauze pad over the stitches, Diego said, "There. I took care of it as you insisted. Now please leave while I clean this up. I don't ever want to see you again."

Without a word of thanks, Evan left the room and headed

down the hall. Diego followed until he saw Evan open the rear door and step outside.

Turning, he returned to the treatment area, cleaned up, and put away his equipment. It took less than five minutes, and everything was back to the way it had been.

Diego checked that his keys were in his pocket, flipped off the light switch, and headed toward the exit.

As he started down the hall, he was startled to see Evan again. For some reason, he'd returned.

"Why are you still here?"

In his surprise, Diego didn't initially notice what his former friend was holding. In his right hand was a Taser, and in the left was a large spray can.

Chapter 24

Evan awoke after another fitful night, having slept very little.

As he sat up, he touched the bandage on his left side and found it dry, with no additional blood loss. It looked as if Diego had done an adequate job.

Looking in the mirror, he saw that his facial damage was mostly healed, but now he had a new injury that set him back. This was another reminder of his failures, and his self-hatred returned.

He headed to the kitchen, took a granola bar from a box on the counter, sat at his dining room table, and began unwrapping it.

There was a spiral-bound notebook on the table, and he looked through it, checking out the addresses of possible targets he'd identified over the last few weeks. He'd spent dozens of hours watching homes, looking for the right locations. There were seven new addresses that he'd written down. Each address connected to someone who either lived alone or was home alone for part of the morning. The locations he chose were single-family homes with fenced-in backyards to conceal his break-in.

He wanted to go after another target quickly to get the failure behind him. Part of him wanted to make another attempt at the woman who'd shot him. He didn't know her name, but the desire to correct his error gnawed at him. She'd be extra cautious now, so waiting to revisit her might be a better choice.

As he contemplated his options, he took a bite of the granola bar, picked up his tablet computer, and pulled up a local news site. He liked to read the stories about his work. He found it satisfying to see the pleas for information and the lack of progress reported for all to see.

Today's article was a bit different. At the end, he saw a photo of the lead investigator, Tucson police detective Dan Felty of the midtown office. The article concluded with a quote from Felty saying, "While this person is quite dangerous, his attacks are cowardly and poorly executed. We recommend extreme vigilance when alone, as this seems to be when he strikes."

Evan slammed the tablet to the table and flung the half-eaten granola bar across the room, where it struck the wall and shattered into chunks. His rage had him physically shaking.

"Cowardly and poorly executed!" he screamed. "I'll show you I'm no coward!"

He lurched up from the table, sending his chair flying, ignoring the pain that the sudden movement caused his wound.

He stormed into his workroom and ripped open the cabinet, trying to decide what approach to take.

Chapter 25

Detectives Felty and Bell pulled in at the midtown office at about 11 am on Monday.

Because of the weekend, there had been a delay in getting Valorie Lee to sit with the sketch artist. Still, she'd arrived early this morning and was now finishing up. The detectives wanted to speak to her again. They hoped there might be something more she remembered since she'd had some time to recover from the trauma. They were also eager to see the sketch and possibly be closer to catching the killer.

Mac got out of the car first and, as she stood, she noticed movement. Turning, she saw someone running towards them from behind a dumpster. He approached from the opposite side of the car and charged toward Dan, who'd only just started to exit the vehicle. The runner had already closed to about 15 feet. He wore a green windbreaker and a bright-blue ski mask and brought up a weapon held in two hands.

"Gun!" Mac screamed as she went for her own weapon.

Mac never heard a shot but did hear Dan yelp as the shooter turned, running away towards the alley, screaming, "Cowards don't hunt cops!"

With her gun in her hand, Mac took off in pursuit of the fleeing man. Aware that Dan was following right behind her.

As Mac ran, it became apparent she wouldn't catch the faster man and that Dan had fallen behind. She glanced over her shoulder and saw him down on the ground.

The voice from ahead yelled to her, "It's him or me. Your choice, Detective!"

Mac dropped to one knee and, for the first time in her career, discharged her weapon at a person. She fired two shots, unsure if either had hit the shooter, then raced back to her fallen friend and partner.

As she approached, she saw his gun on the ground next to him, and a four-inch dart clutched in his left hand.

"No! Go get him!" Dan commanded in a weak voice.

Instead, Mac dropped to his side and pulled out her phone to call the dispatch center. Never in all her years on the department did she feel the level of panic that threatened to overwhelm her now.

"Hi, Mac. What…"

She cut the dispatcher off, "Midtown detective bureau, back alley. Officer down. I need an ambulance now!"

She set the phone down, leaving the call connected, and focused on Dan. She forced him on to his back. "Dan, open your eyes; stay awake!" she said urgently. He didn't respond.

Checking, Mac could tell that, for the moment, his breathing hadn't stopped, but it was slow and shallow.

Less than 20 seconds later, she heard the sound of running feet, lots of them. She glanced towards the building entrance and saw a wave of people pouring out of the building, racing toward her.

"Get a resuscitation kit and several doses of Narcan, fast!" she yelled.

A couple of people in the crowd peeled off the get the equipment needed. The rest of them ran up.

One of the first to arrive secured Dan's gun from the ground.

"Someone get me an evidence bag for this dart," a voice said.

"They're getting the equipment now, Mac. What else?"

She glanced up and saw Lieutenant Miller. "It's been less than a minute. He might still be close. Green jacket and a bright-blue ski mask. I fired twice, not sure if I hit him."

"Keep breathing, Dan. Keep breathing," she said, oblivious to the radio transmissions going out from the group with the attacker's description. Nor was she aware that half of those in the crowd were now sprinting back the way they'd come to get in their cars to go look for the shooter.

Moments later, Mac noticed what she'd been watching for.

"Where's the equipment? He stopped breathing!" Mac yelled as she leaned over Dan's head and put her mouth over his, pushing air into his oxygen-starved lungs.

Others were approaching, and she moved aside as her fellow officers arrived, bringing the lifesaving equipment. A tube attached an oxygen tank to a football-sized bag with a mask on it. Someone placed the mask on Dan's face, and the operator began squeezing the bag and pushing nearly pure oxygen into his lungs.

A uniformed officer pushed his way in and pressed an auto-injector into Dan's left shoulder, delivering a dose of the opioid-combating Narcan.

Another female detective pulled out a folding knife and swiftly sliced the front of Dan's shirt wide open, exposing the chest so the pads for the automated external defibrillator (AED) could be applied.

The device was activated, and a frighteningly slow heart rate appeared on the built-in ECG screen. The machine would automatically shock the detective's heart back into a normal rhythm if called for. But the current heart activity didn't call for defibrillation.

An officer injected another dose of Narcan into the unconscious detective's thigh as they heard rapidly approaching sirens. Seconds later, a large rescue squad and an ambulance from the fire department arrived, and the paramedics hurried in to take over.

A female medic asked, "What happened?"

Mac answered, "He was injected with 10 milliliters of pure medical-grade carfentanil. We were told this dose would drop an elephant."

"Medical-grade? Are you sure?"

"Yeah, stolen from a zoo," Mac said.

"Interesting," the medic commented.

As she spoke, the medic lay on her belly at Dan's head and placed a metal L-shaped device in Dan's mouth and used it to raise his tongue and jaw so she could see down his throat to install the tube into his trachea.

The other medic started an IV in the right arm and injected medications into it.

One of the firefighters reported, "His blood pressure is 58/40, and his pulse is only 46."

"We'll work on those in the truck," said one of the medics calmly.

"How's his breathing?" Lieutenant Miller asked.

"He isn't, but that's not a problem. Since the tube is in, we have full control of his respiratory system. The blood pressure and slow heart rate are a concern. So we'll give him medications on the way in, which will bring both up," the medic explained as they moved Dan to the stretcher and loaded him into the back of the red-and-white ambulance.

Chapter 26

Evan ran as fast as possible, aware that the short female detective was behind him. He shouted a final taunt in her direction and heard two gunshots. Neither hit him, but he saw a chunk of wood blasted off the side of a telephone pole he passed. The near miss caused him to stumble, and he felt sutures in his side rip free. He yelped in pain but noticed he no longer heard the footsteps pursuing him.

Glancing over his shoulder, Evan saw her running back to her partner, the man who'd called him a coward in the article. He'd collapsed to the ground, and Evan smiled, knowing what the dose of carfentanil was doing. He also knew he wasn't in the clear yet. There'd soon be many more officers chasing him down.

Evan didn't know if the attack would kill Detective Felty. He suspected there was a chance he'd get medical care in time, but that didn't matter. The attack aimed to correct the impression that he was a coward.

Evan wasn't a coward – after this, they'd know it and give him the respect he deserved.

Making a few more turns, he stopped behind a bar that hadn't yet opened for the day. He went to the rear of the building and leaned against the back wall, waiting for his breathing to return to normal. Then he removed the green jacket he wore. Underneath, he had on a nearly empty drawstring backpack. Opening it, he removed glasses and a new ball cap with the Diamondbacks' logo and put them on, stuffing the jacket and ski mask inside the pack.

Next, Evan checked his wound, which had started bleeding again. He removed the bandage and saw almost half of the sutures had ripped out with all his running. His fury at Diego's poor suturing overtook the excitement he'd been feeling.

He re-dressed the wound using old napkins from the bottom of the backpack because he hadn't brought any bandages. He then took a length of duct tape from the roll he'd brought and covered the wound. He needed to keep attention off the site of the injury.

Putting the backpack on, he then casually walked three blocks to a laundromat, listening as he heard sirens in the area.

Once inside, he went to a specific washing machine and glanced inside at the blanket he'd put there several hours earlier. He added more money and let the blanket wash a second time as he sat near the back of the room, facing the street. If the police came in looking for their suspect, the blanket would explain his reason for being here.

By the time the blanket had been washed again and eventually dried, he could safely leave the laundromat. The frantic hunt for him would have moved away.

Chapter 27

Mac had been pacing the nearly empty emergency department waiting room for the last 30 minutes, anxious for news. As she turned, she saw a uniformed figure approaching. Instinctively she stood a little taller and took in a breath as Deputy Chief of Detectives Mike Sawyer walked in.

"Hello, Chief."

"Detective. Any news?"

"No, still waiting. He got a dose that could stop an elephant. This is bad, real bad," Mac said with a quiver in her voice.

Nodding, the chief said, "From what I heard, the only reason he's alive is because of your quick actions."

Shaking her head, Mac said, "Everyone in the building responded. They all get the credit. If it hadn't happened right there, he'd be dead. All I did was call for help.

"You know, when I ran back to Dan, he was almost unconscious, and he tried to order me to leave him and chase the shooter."

The deputy chief smiled. "Sounds like you had to make a tough choice."

Mac nodded.

"Well, you did the right thing," he assured her, then, pausing, he added, "I thought Lieutenant Miller would be here by now."

"He went to get Dan's wife, Abby. He didn't want her driving herself," Mac explained.

The two of them sat, and Mac answered the few questions the chief had for her.

Minutes later, Lieutenant Miller came in, leading a medium-built redheaded woman. She went directly to Mac.

"What've you heard?" Abby asked with a quivering voice.

Mac stood and instinctively wanted to reach out and hug the terrified woman but knew her touch wouldn't be welcome.

"We haven't been told anything yet. He's drugged and unconscious. They're breathing for him. But his heart never stopped."

"How long was he down, not breathing?" Dan's wife asked the woman she resented. The fear in her voice evident.

"Seconds only. They were running to us with the resuscitation kit when he stopped. His brain was never deprived of oxygen."

Abby nodded, and Mac saw a little of the terror fade.

"Have a seat, Abby, and I'll tell you anything I can," Mac told her partner's wife.

Nodding, the redhead sat and said, "Please, tell me what happened."

For several minutes, Mac told her the entire story. When she finished, Lieutenant Miller added, "Mrs. Felty, I was there, too. Mac here is certainly the reason Dan's still alive."

Abby cried harder before being able to speak. "For two-and-a-half years, I have hated the fact you're the woman he spends so many weekends and holidays with instead of being home with his family," she eventually managed between sobs.

Mac nodded, all too aware of the other woman's feelings.

"I'm so glad it was you with him today," the distraught wife added.

Hesitantly, Mac reached out and took the other woman's hand, expecting her to pull it away, but instead, Abby squeezed back and didn't let go.

Fifteen minutes later, a short Hispanic nurse walked up. "Is one of you, Mrs. Felty?" she asked.

"Yes. I am," Abby said.

"You can come back now," the nurse said.

Abby stood and started to follow, then stopped and looked back at Mac. "You're coming, too," she told her.

As Mac stood, the nurse looked as if she was about to object but changed her mind. She swiped the badge clipped at her waist, allowing the doors to part, giving the three of them access to the emergency department.

They passed by more than a dozen exam areas divided by sliding curtains. At the back of the department were four large rooms containing advanced equipment for the more critical patients. The nurse led the women to one of them. Before opening the door, the nurse stopped and prepared them, "This'll be a bit disturbing. There are lots of wires, tubes, and machines."

The women nodded. Both had seen things like this before.

The nurse opened the door, and they stepped inside.

Dan lay in a hospital bed, wearing a white gown with a blue print. A white sheet covered most of his body. The endotracheal tube the paramedics had inserted was still in his mouth. However, it was now attached to other long tubes, which led to a four-foot-tall ventilator that stood next to the bed. The machine pushed a finely tuned volume of oxygen into his lungs 14 times each minute.

On the opposite side of the bed sat a similar-sized machine. It pumped the blood from an artery in Dan's arm, ran it through the machine, and then returned it to his body.

Several computer monitors were on the wall displaying oxygen saturation, vital signs, and an EKG, among many other things Mac didn't understand.

Four IV bags of different sizes were at the head of the bed. They dripped their contents into tubing that Mac assumed connected to a vein in her partner's arm under the sheet.

Each of the machines made one kind of sound or another, and the cacophony was unnerving.

As they were taking in the sight, someone else entered the room. They turned and saw a man with Middle-Eastern features wearing a white lab coat. He seemed to Mac to be quite young.

"Mrs. Felty?"

"That's me, and this is Mackenzie, Dan's partner."

Nodding to the women, he said, "I'm Doctor Kabeer. I'm the senior resident assigned to your husband's case."

Abby shook the man's hand as Mac tried to stay in the background. She appreciated being included, but this moment belonged to Abby.

"Your husband is very fortunate. He received care quickly, and the paramedics stabilized his vitals before any obvious damage happened. There's a bit more to it than this but, in general, we'll continue what the medics started and keep his vitals stable until the drug wears off. It was a massive dose, and that'll take a while. We'll be admitting him to the ICU so we can monitor him until his condition is stable. Does this make sense so far?"

"Yes, I understand," Abby said.

The doctor continued, "Good. There are a couple of concerns. We need to make sure his kidney and liver functions stay healthy since there's a toxin in his system. We're monitoring them with frequent blood tests, and, so far, they're okay.

"Now the ventilator will keep him alive until he can breathe on his own, and the dialysis machine is cleaning the toxins from his blood. Do you have any questions?"

"How long until he wakes up?" Abby asked.

With a hesitant voice, the doctor answered, "It's impossible to tell, but I expect it will be in the next 12 to 24 hours, if things go well."

Abby looked at Mac to see if she had any questions.

"I know there're still lots of unknowns, but do you see anything at this point to indicate any permanent damage?" Mac asked.

"In general, all the tests have come back okay. I don't see anything now, but that could all change," Dr. Kabeer explained.

Chapter 28

MAC HAD EXCUSED HERSELF, LEAVING ABBY FELTY WITH HER comatose husband, and returned to the waiting room.

Her two superior officers looked up as she approached, and then she took the seat between them.

"That was awful. There are machines and tubes. Some were breathing for him, and others were sucking out his blood and cleaning it and putting it back. The doctor said his blood-work is good, and there are no obvious long-term issues, but things can still change. Hopefully, he'll wake up in 12 to 24 hours."

"I guess that's as good as we can hope for," Deputy Chief Sawyer said, while considering the information he'd heard.

Lieutenant Miller nodded in silent agreement.

"Detective, let's step outside where we can talk privately," the deputy chief said.

Leaving the hospital, the three law-enforcement officers stepped into the hot midday air. They headed to a small covered pavilion with a couple of picnic tables under it. It looked like this outside area was for hospital employees to take a break or eat lunch. No one else was there, and the three gathered around a table.

The deputy chief looked at Mac and said, "I hear the FBI has offered their services. I understand the reluctance to bring them in, and I share it. But with the senior detective on the case in the hospital and, as long as this has been going on, I'm starting to think it might make sense to take them up on their offer."

Shaking her head, Mac said, "Not yet, Sir! Please. We've got several strong leads that we need to follow up on. A composite sketch of the attacker was made just this morning. We were on our way to see it when Dan was drugged. Also, we have the lot number for the spray foam. That should allow us to track it, hopefully to the person who bought it. I also learned the lab results are back on a fragment of a rubber glove left at an earlier scene. Again, this may allow us to track him. I also need to follow up with a sheriff's deputy in Montana who apparently had a similar incident."

"If there was an out-of-state attack, then this is already a matter for the FBI," Chief Sawyer stated.

Nodding, Mac said, "True, but the victim there was a cow, not a human. The FBI knows about it and hasn't said anything yet."

When she finished, Mac hoped she hadn't missed anything that could help swing the chief's decision.

"Sir," Lieutenant Miller added, "Mac's right, we've got lots of new evidence to follow up on, and if we bring the FBI in, we'll lose the momentum we have. I can assist her until detective Felty is back on his feet."

After thinking about it, the chief nodded, looked at the lieutenant, and answered, "All right. But I want an inter-agency task force set up immediately. Get two more detectives assigned, and I'll get a resource from the sheriff's department. I understand one of the early attacks was in their jurisdiction. Detective Bell will head this up with you guiding as needed."

Turning his gaze to Mac, he asked, "Can you lead a task force, Detective?"

"Yes, Sir. I can do this," Mac answered with wide eyes.

"Good. I know you're worried about your partner, but now is the time to hunt the person who did this to him. Let's have everyone in place by 8 am tomorrow and get this solved."

"Chief, do I have permission to send someone from the task force to Montana? I want face-to-face interviews. Not by phone or on a video call," the new task force lead said.

"You have permission to do anything needed," the deputy chief told Mac.

The three of them rose and headed toward their vehicles. Mac hated leaving while Dan's condition remained critical, but she knew he'd want her working and not sitting around.

Chapter 29

Jenny Moore and her husband, Bob, walked down the sidewalk. Each was holding the leash of a dog. The twin 70-pound mutts had been part of the family for four years, and the evening walks through the subdivision were a regular event.

As they were approaching their house, Jenny's phone rang. Fishing it from her pocket while holding the leash, she answered, "Hello?"

"Detective Moore? This is Deputy Chief Mike Sawyer."

After a brief pause of confusion, Jenny replied, "Good evening, Chief. What can I do for you?"

"I wanted to call and let you know that, effective immediately, you and your partner are being assigned to an inter-agency task force to work on the spray foam case."

She felt a thrill. This was the biggest case in a decade, and everyone in the department wanted to be involved in the high-profile investigation.

"Excellent, Chief. I'll be glad to help in any way I can. I assume my lieutenant's been informed?"

"Yes, Lieutenant Miller is with me now and is on the phone with your partner. This all came about quickly, so I offered to give him a hand, making calls," the deputy chief explained.

"Sounds good. Who's running the task force?"

"You will be reporting to Mackenzie Bell."

The thrill of being involved withered a bit as she fought to keep the irritation from her voice. "Sir, she's pretty low on the seniority list to lead a task force," the senior detective commented.

"Maybe, but she knows the case better than anyone, and I have confidence in her. I need you to work with her and do what you can to help her bring this case to a close as soon as possible."

Understanding that the last sentence was a gentle warning against letting Mac's lower seniority be an issue, Jenny replied, "Yes, Sir. I'll do everything I can."

Everyone had heard what had happened to Dan Felty, and Jenny knew that Mac's familiarity with the case might make her the best choice, but it still didn't sit well. However, she'd interacted with Mac before and liked her. She'd make sure to get rid of her reservations and make the situation work.

"Good. Mac will be calling you soon. She's sending you out of town for a few days. I'll let her explain, but you might want to start packing. She wants you on a flight first thing in the morning."

Jenny's stomach dropped. Her excitement about being assigned to the task force had turned to dread.

"Yes, sir. I'll expect the call."

The deputy chief disconnected, and Bob looked at her and asked, "What was that about?"

"It looks like I'll be going out of town for a few days," the detective told her husband.

As they got home and unleashed the dogs, Jenny relayed the news to Bob, leaving out her displeasure of having to report to a junior detective.

An hour later, as she finished packing a suitcase, her phone rang again, and she saw Mackenzie's name on the screen.

"Hey, Mac," she answered.

"Hi Jenny, I understand the chief called you?"

"He gave me the basics. Where am I going?"

"Montana."

"What's in Montana?"

"Dead cows. Let me start at the beginning," Mac said.

As the story progressed, it got worse. She had an early morning flight to Montana by way of Seattle. She had to be at the airport extra early to deal with the red tape regarding transporting her gun in her checked luggage.

After her flight landed, she'd have a five-hour drive to a ranch in the middle of nowhere so that she could investigate the murder of cows.

Mac had been kind on the phone, apologizing for the time of the flight. And she personally explained the details of the case before sending a copy of the case files to her email so she could review them on the plane.

Mac's attitude had taken some of the sting out of the situation, but it couldn't fix the fact that Jenny was terrified of flying.

Chapter 30

Mac ARRIVED AT WORK AN HOUR EARLY THE FOLLOWING DAY. As the task force commander, she wanted to get things in order before the rest of her team arrived.

When Lieutenant Miller walked in, he found her at her desk, staring at the composite drawing of their suspect.

"Morning, Mac. Is that the sketch from yesterday?"

"Yeah, it is. Take a look. It's not very good," she said as she handed the sketch to her boss.

The lieutenant stared at the image for several seconds before answering. "Well, this is about as generic as it gets. There's nothing about him that stands out."

"I know. It might not help as much as I hoped," Mac said.

"Mac, you need to know there has been another attack. It happened over the weekend."

"When, where? Why wasn't I notified?"

"It was about an hour north of here in a veterinary office. It was closed for the weekend, and when the staff came in yesterday, they found an employee dead. I spoke to the local sheriff, and he verified the foam and Taser," Lieutenant Miller explained.

"Something about that doesn't feel right," Mac said. "He hasn't attacked that far away and never in a business before."

Agreeing, the lieutenant said, "True, but this is the second time veterinary medicine has touched this case. First the stolen drugs and then this atypical attack."

"Was anything stolen from the vet's office?" Mac asked.

"No. Nothing was disturbed. Just the dead employee."

As they were speaking, two others entered the room. The first was Tom Koster. When he saw the others, he said, "Morning, LT, Mac."

"Hey, Tom. Are you going to be okay for a couple of days without your partner?" Miller asked.

Detective Tom Koster laughed. "I'll be fine, but she might not be. Jenny hates flying. She called me earlier, grumbling about dead cows in Montana."

The man who entered with Tom looked to be in his late fifties and gave them all a quizzical look. He wore a grey polo shirt with the Pima County Sheriff Department logo.

Lieutenant Miller approached him and held out his hand. "I assume you're Detective George Jenkins? I'm Tony Miller. I'm the supervisor of the Midtown Detective Bureau."

The two shook hands, and Lieutenant Miller continued, "I believe you already know Detective Mackenzie Bell. She's the task force leader."

The newcomer and Mac nodded to one another, and the older man said, "Yeah, she's been keeping me updated on the case. Thanks for including me on the team."

Mac replied, "We're glad to have you. We've got lots of leads to track down and not enough resources. We're taking over a conference room down the hall and will use it for the duration of the case. Grab some coffee or whatever you need and meet me there in five. I'll start the briefing then."

Several minutes later, they gathered in the conference room, and Mac began her presentation. She spent almost 20 minutes reviewing the case, all 10 attacks, and where the investigation stood.

She then went to the whiteboard and wrote each of their names and assignments.

"Jenkins, you have the FoamX. Are you familiar with the product?"

"No, this is the first time I've heard of it."

"Look it up online. There are several videos out there. Then work on tracing the lot number we found on the can," Mac instructed.

"Will do, Boss."

She then continued, "Tom, take the composite drawing of the suspect and the DNA profile and see if you can find a match. Look outside of Arizona too. Certainly include Montana and text a copy of the drawing to your partner. It might be helpful to her as she speaks to the rancher."

"I'm on it," the detective agreed.

"Before you start, talk to Lieutenant Miller. There was another attack the other day. It was out of our jurisdiction. Follow up on it and see what you can learn. It doesn't meet the pattern we've seen."

"I'll take care of it," Tom stated.

Nodding, Mac said, "Now that we finally have the analysis of the rubber glove fragment we found at an early scene, I'll be running with that. See if I can determine a brand and where it's sold."

They all had their assignments, and Mac was eager to start looking into the glove but had something to take care of first. She needed to call Abby Felty to find out how her partner was doing.

Chapter 31

Awareness slowly returned, and with it, Dan Felty's eyes opened for the first time in more than 24 hours. He was lethargic and a thick fog clouded his mind. He wasn't sure where he was and wanted to go back to sleep.

Then, without warning and outside his control, a blast of air suddenly forced itself into his lungs, startling him. He tried to resist the sudden intrusion but was unable to. When it finished, he tried to take another breath on his own, but it was restricted, and he fought against the machine.

Panic built, and the two adrenal glands adjacent to his kidneys released their contents. The fight or flight hormone coursed through his system. His heart rate increased, and his level of alertness improved. He became aware of the tube in his mouth and wanted it out immediately. He made an unconscious attempt to grab it only to find his hands were tied, and he could only get them halfway to his face. Now his terror increased, and he started thrashing. He became aware of an alarm sounding, then heard a voice, "Dan! Stop! You need to lie still and try to relax."

He knew the voice and focused his attention on the face of his wife, Abby, who stood at the bedside in the dimly lit room.

This calmed him some and he stopped moving. Then he noticed Mac standing at Abby's side, and his confusion returned.

Where was he? Why couldn't he move his arms? He wondered.

Suddenly the machine to his left made a noise, and air again pushed its way into his lungs. Again, he tried to fight it but was unable.

This time it was Mac who spoke. Her tone was commanding. "Dan! Don't fight it. You're on a ventilator. Relax and breathe with the machine. Not against it."

He glared at her.

Smiling, Mac said, "Don't look at me like that. Just breathe with the machine and you'll be okay."

The next time the machine cycled, Dan allowed it to fill his lungs and found he could control his exhalation.

A blinding illumination filled the room, startling him. He squinted as an unknown female face came into view in the now brightly lit room.

"He just woke up," he heard Abby say.

"That's good," the newcomer said as she went to the ventilator and silenced the alarm. Turning to the bed, she said, "Mr. Felty. I'm Janice, your nurse. I need you to relax and let the vent do the breathing."

Dan raised his left arm, but it stopped when the strap restraining it reached its limit. He gave it a gentle extra tug.

Nodding, Janice said, "I know. You don't like the restraints. I understand, but we can't have you grabbing at the tube in your mouth. If you were to yank it out, you might permanently damage your vocal cords."

Dan forced a look of annoyance to his face, which Janice ignored.

She returned to the machine and adjusted the settings.

"Now, I changed a setting on the vent. It will still breathe for you every six seconds, but you can now take extra breaths on your own if needed. Work with it and not against it."

Dan experimented, taking in a breath on his own, and immediately felt a sense of relief.

"See? That's good. Try to relax. If the ventilator causes you too much distress, we can sedate you, but we'd rather not. We want you waking up. I'll let the doctor know you're awake. Hopefully, the tube can come out soon."

Janice turned and left the room.

Dan still felt confused. He glanced around the room and saw a wall clock. It said it was 11:15. He looked at the window and, even with the blinds closed, he could tell it was dark outside.

He looked at the two women and frowned to express his confusion.

Abby took his hand and Mac said, "Do you remember what happened?"

Dan shook his head.

"We were working. When we got to the station, the spray foam killer was waiting for us, and he shot you with a carfentanil dart."

For a moment, the words didn't make much sense, then something in his mind snapped open, and everything came rushing back.

"I think he remembers," Abby said.

Dan nodded.

With his hand, Dan acted out holding a pen and writing

A pen and paper sat on the counter on the other side of the room, and Mac got them and handed them to Abby, who helped her husband hold the pad and scribble out his first question.

"Did you catch him?"

"No, not yet," Mac replied.

"How long?" he wrote.

"How long have you been here? Almost a day and a half," Abby told him.

Dan wrote out a few other questions and then became tired and needed to sleep. Before drifting off, he heard Mac say, "I need to get going. It'll be another long day tomorrow, and I need a little sleep."

"I understand. Thanks for being here, and be careful. We don't need you ending up here, too," Abby said.

"I will. Please let me know when he's off the ventilator."

Then something happened that startled Dan as much as any of what he'd recently experienced. His wife embraced Mac with sincere concern.

Before he fell asleep, and as Mac left the room, Dan wondered what had happened between these women that he'd missed.

Chapter 32

THE TUCSON ANIMAL SHELTER WAS A LARGE BUILDING ON THE city's outskirts. It stood at the back of an industrial park, where the constant barking of the residents wouldn't disturb anyone.

Sadly the pet adoption rate was half of what the intake was, which meant new arrivals had a short, three-week window to be adopted before being euthanized.

This fact broke the hearts of the employees who worked tirelessly to find homes for as many animals as possible.

For the last couple of years, most of the staff had been thankful for one particular co-worker. It wasn't that they especially liked Evan Brown. In fact, most of them didn't like him at all. He never socialized and was a bit awkward to be around. However, he dealt with the termination and disposal of the animals that weren't adoptable or had been at the shelter for the maximum amount of time.

Before Evan arrived a couple of years ago, most employees needed to be involved in the horrendous task from time to time. Now, Evan did it by himself and, at the end of the day, the others could go home not feeling guilty about the work they did.

At first, his co-workers were concerned because the new employee seemed enthusiastic about his work, but over time that had faded. He now kept to himself in the back room and did his job without complaining.

Usually, Evan worked evenings, so his duties wouldn't be noticeable to anyone stopping in to possibly adopt an animal. This morning, he arrived at work very early. There was only one other car in the employee parking area, a red Honda. He recognized it as belonging to the facility manager, Amber. She was nice enough to him, but that didn't keep Evan from smiling as he fantasized about shooting her with a Taser and foaming her.

Subconsciously, he glanced up to the corner of the roof and at the security camera perched there. That was all it took to kill the fantasy. Evan was intelligent and knew he would eventually be caught, but it wouldn't be from doing something stupid, like being on camera where he killed.

His early arrival wasn't because of his work but rather the need to do something about the bullet wound in his side. It still bled a day after he'd accidentally ripped out some of the sutures. Since going back to his friend Diego wasn't an option, he'd need to make do the best he could.

The animal shelter had a limited on-site medical clinic available to care for the animals and contained the supplies he needed. The two vet techs who worked there were always a little late, so he'd have all the time he needed to get himself patched up. This wouldn't be the first time he'd raided the clinic for personal use.

He approached the rear employee entrance and the door clicked open as he waved his employee ID card in front of the scanner.

As he entered, he was assaulted by the sounds of the non-stop barking and wondered how many of them he'd be silencing permanently later today.

Evan had initially taken the job, hoping it would feed his

hunger to kill and, for more than a year, it had worked. But the deaths were so peaceful that it wasn't what he needed. He liked his job and the peace it provided, but, over time, his work stopped satisfying his need, and he began to plan to obtain the answers he craved. Those answers would only come from the right kind of human deaths.

He passed his work area and entered the clinic, where the lights snapped on as he arrived. He went to the equipment cabinets along the back wall and retrieved bandages, tape, disinfectant, antibiotic ointment, and a bottle of Clot Now bleeding control for animals.

Not wanting to get blood on his hands, he looked and spotted the box of Tough Finger brand rubber gloves and pulled on a pair of large latex gloves. Next, he removed his shirt and pulled off the duct tape, holding the bloody paper towels in place. Some of the blood had dried, and the paper had adhered to his skin. As he pulled it away, he inadvertently pulled the wound partially open again, and the bleeding resumed. Fortunately, Diego's work to cauterize the blood vessels stopped most of the bleeding.

Taking a small towel from a drawer, he soaked it in the disinfectant and began cleaning the site of the injury. Even before he started, he knew it would be agonizing. He fought not to scream as the fiery pain erupted. Forcing himself to finish quickly, he took the nozzle from the Clot Now, pressed it deep into the bullet wound, and squeezed the bottle. The fine powder blasted outward and, on contact with the moisture in the blood, hardened to create a barrier and stop the bleeding.

Feeling light-headed from the pain and with sweat on his face, Evan grabbed the exam table to steady himself and waited for the pain to subside.

When it eventually did, he continued by applying the antibiotic ointment and dressing the wound using the bandages.

With the wound as well taken care of as possible, Evan

cleaned up his mess, not wanting anyone to question what he'd done. He needed to get through his shift and return home. He'd already picked out a new target.

Chapter 33

BENJAMIN WILCOX YAWNED AS HE STEPPED OUT OF HIS HOME into the already warm early morning air.

It was a little after 5 am, and the temperature was already 74 degrees. It would be close to 100 again today.

The sun had only started to reduce the darkness of the night as the elderly man started heading down the street on foot, as he did several times a week. He turned on to Grove Street and, right on time, he saw the door to a house he was approaching open, and a woman about his age emerged.

Seeing her brought an unconscious smile to his face.

He waited as she approached. "Good morning Peg," he said.

With a smile of her own, Peggy Brill fell into step next to him, and the two continued down the street.

As the pair took their first steps, Peggy gently pressed her shoulder against his, and they both sighed at the only physical affection they ever shared.

"Hi, Benny. I was afraid you might cancel on me again."

"No. I'm feeling better today. I didn't want to cancel Tuesday, but I wasn't sure what I might be coming down with and didn't want to pass it on to you."

Benny and Peg had been friends for several decades. When their spouses were alive, the couples often traveled together as the families were very close. When the time had come to retire, the families had all made sure to get homes in the same subdivision.

Now that they were both widowed and in their early eighties, Benny and Peg relied on each other for friendship and support. While there was nothing romantic about their relationship, their friendship was on the level of what they'd shared with their spouses.

The two walked for several blocks without saying anything else. Some mornings they talked the whole time while walking. On others, the friends were almost silent, enjoying each other's company as they got in their exercise for the day.

Suddenly Peg came to a stop. "Look! Next to that house!"

Benny looked where she was pointing. While his eyesight had somewhat deteriorated, he could still make out a person moving in the dark next to the house they were about to pass.

Watching, the couple saw as the person disappeared around the back.

Looking at the residence, they noticed no lights were on and no cars were parked in the driveway.

In the still of the early morning, they heard the faint sound of something breaking. The sound could have come from behind the house, but they couldn't be sure.

"We should call the police," Peg said.

Benny inwardly cringed, not wanting to be the kooky old man who called the police for something that turned out not to be a problem. At the same time, he wasn't going to walk away and pretend he hadn't seen something.

"No, not yet. I'll go check it out."

"That could be dangerous."

"It'll be fine. You stay here, and I'll be back in a minute," Benny said as he headed towards the house, following the route the strange figure took.

He worked his way around the side and to the rear of the building, peering into the backyard for several seconds, looking for the person he and Peg had seen.

When he saw no one, he continued, noticing the rear door. He could tell it had been forced open as the frame was damaged and the door ajar.

The temptation to go in was almost overwhelming. Almost, but Benny wasn't a fool, and he turned around and headed back toward his walking companion while digging his phone out of his pocket.

"You had me scared! Did you find anything?" Peg asked, relieved to have her friend back on the road with her.

"Someone forced the back door open. That's what we heard. I'm calling the police now," Benny explained.

Chapter 34

OFFICER BILL RICHARDS SAT BEHIND THE WHEEL OF HIS POLICE
cruiser, snacking on smoked walnuts.

The evening had started out busy but had quieted down
after 1 am. He hoped it would stay this way for another 20
minutes until his shift was over.

"Three-eight and three-nine," the voice on the radio
said.

As he reached for his radio, he heard Donna Kerney's
voice reply, "Three-nine."

Responding as well, Bill said into the microphone, "Three-
eight."

"Three-eight and three-nine, possible home invasion in
progress, 1126 Grove Street, just south of Pinewood. Caller
reports seeing someone in the yard, and the back door has
been forced open."

Both responding officers acknowledged the instructions
and, with emergency lights activated, raced to the scene,
approaching from different directions.

As Bill pulled up, he saw Donna was already there and was
exiting her cruiser. He stopped the car, got out, and followed
her to an elderly couple standing on the street.

By the time he got to them, the witnesses were finishing explaining what they'd seen.

Looking at Bill, Donna said, "Sounds like the rear door was forced."

She returned her attention to the couple, "We'll go have a look. Please stay here."

The officers made their way around to the rear of the residence. They saw the situation was exactly as the elderly man had described.

Bill squeezed the microphone at his collar and said, "Three-eight."

"Go ahead, Three-eight."

"Confirming the rear door has been forced open. Three-eight and nine are going in."

"Understood. Three-eight and nine making entry at 0542."

Drawing his gun, Bill entered through the door with Donna following behind.

Stepping into the dark house, they couldn't see much and Bill felt his heart racing as they entered the unknown situation.

Donna clicked on her flashlight, saying, "This is the Tuscon Police Department. We're coming in!"

There was no reply, and the house was completely quiet, but there was the slight scent of cooked food.

The officers proceeded through the home with their weapons sweeping left and right in front of them. Their lights illuminating every room as they searched. After clearing the kitchen and living room, they went through the three bedrooms, even checking under the beds and in the closets.

As the officers were finishing up, they were aware of a vehicle pulling into the driveway.

"Sounds like the homeowner is here," Donna said as she holstered her weapon.

"Why don't you go talk to them, and I'll check the garage? That's the only place we haven't looked," Bill said.

"We might go home on time, after all," Donna replied, smiling as she headed for the front door.

Bill went to the only door coming off the hall they hadn't yet explored, opened it, and stepped into the garage.

Not air-conditioned, the garage was about 30 degrees warmer than the house, the previous day's heat not having fully dissipated. The homeowner stored their trash can in here, giving the room a foul odor.

Finding the light switch, he turned it on, illuminating the space. There were numerous items near the center of the room, making it clear that the space was for storage, not vehicle parking. Along one wall was a washer and dryer and a chest freezer. Along the other wall were large shelves holding a dozen or more matching totes, all with labels.

After a quick glance around the room, Bill turned the lights off and closed the door between the house and the garage.

"Nothing here. Let's go home," he muttered to himself as he headed out to catch up with Donna. He was thankful there'd been no one hiding inside. The paperwork would be much simpler than if they'd made an arrest.

As he got outside, he saw Donna collecting information from a middle age man who, it turned out, lived here alone and was returning home from working all night.

Approaching the pair, Donna said, "Mr. Dexter, this is Officer Richards. He and I checked the house, and it looks like whoever broke in must have fled when we first arrived. Other than the back door, there's no sign of any damage. You'll want to check and make sure nothing is missing."

The officers spoke to the homeowner for a few more minutes and then departed the scene.

Fifteen minutes later, in the dark garage, the lid of the chest freezer rose. A nearly frozen man pulled himself up on to the front edge and collapsed over the side, dropping in a heap on the concrete floor. A Taser pistol fell from his numb grip.

Evan lay on the floor of the 86-degree garage, thankful for its warmth. He'd been in the freezer for almost half an hour, terrified he'd run out of air. It would be twice as long before he was warm enough to carry out the task that had brought him here.

As he lay on the floor, he smiled at the idea that had entered his twisted mind.

Chapter 35

Two days later, at 4 am, Evan crawled out of bed. After working the evening before, he'd spent several hours driving through selected neighborhoods, looking for new targets.

On his tablet, he could access county records and get an idea of how many people lived at specific addresses. Then he'd make sure that there was only a single car at the home. When he felt reasonably confident he'd found a potential target, he'd loiter in the neighborhood for a couple of days, watching the activity.

He slowly passed a house on Kinder Avenue. He needed to make sure no one was home. If things happened as expected, a pickup truck would return within 20 minutes.

The home was dark and there were no cars in the drive. Evan had already verified that the homeowner used the garage for storage and not parking, so there probably wasn't another driver-age person living there. Continuing up the road, he pulled over and stopped, watching his mirrors.

As expected, a blue Chevy pickup truck pulled in several minutes later. Smiling, the killer made a notation in the spiral-bound notebook on the seat next to him. The final step was to return in the night and get a final look at the property. Once he'd confirmed the address, he'd return in a few days and would be waiting in the house when the homeowner arrived.

He now had a little more than an hour to get across town. Today's target arrived home from her morning walk between 6 am and 6:15, and Evan planned to be in the home waiting when she did.

The early morning traffic was light, and Evan felt almost giddy as he arrived and stopped in the parking lot of a closed restaurant a quarter of a mile from the house.

Slipping on his pack, he locked the car and headed out with the green ball cap positioned to hide his face.

Twenty minutes later, his destination became visible. He approached the house from the rear of the subdivision and entered the backyard. Today wasn't the first time he'd been here. A week ago, he'd investigated the house as a possible target at night, looking for signs of dogs or alarm systems. There were none.

He checked his watch and saw that he had about 10 minutes before the woman who lived here would arrive. Not wanting to take a chance on an early return, Evan went to the side of the building that was least visible from the neighboring properties. He smashed a bedroom window using a brick he'd placed under the window on his reconnaissance visit.

Using the side of the brick, he swiped the remaining jagged glass shards from the frame, then used his arms to hoist himself up the four feet to the window and went in head first. He landed awkwardly but quickly got back on his feet and determined he was in a bedroom.

Evan's eyes were adjusting to the dark when he heard a sound in the house, and his heart rate increased. He wasn't alone. Maybe the woman who lived here hadn't taken her walk or had come home early. Either way, he needed to move quickly. Even now, a call to 911 could be going out after the sound of the glass breaking.

He headed toward the bedroom door with the Taser in his

hand, thinking about his still-fresh bullet wound and not wanting another.

As he reached the door, he sensed someone approaching and prepared to fire.`

The other was coming in low and fast and, when Evan fired, he missed.

A low, menacing growl came from a large creature in front of him. In the dark, it reminded him of a small bear.

The animal continued to approach, and Evan retreated, aware that he was being pursued.

As he dived head-first out of the window, his forearm scraped a small remaining piece of glass in the window frame.

He landed in a heap, with all his weight coming down on his shoulder. The pain instantly took his breath away, but he got back on his feet and ran, infuriated by another failure.

Chapter 36

DAN FELTY WALKED INTO THE BEDROOM. HIS HAIR WAS WET, and he had a towel wrapped around his waist.

As he dressed, he noted how it felt good to shower and put on clean clothes. He felt thankful to do these simple tasks without anyone hovering over him. Since getting home from the hospital the night before, either Abby or one of the kids had been with him constantly, and he felt smothered.

His strength and mental focus were nearly back to normal, and he needed to be active, not sitting around. While mostly recovered, he still had a dull ache in his upper arm where the dart had struck and a scratchy sensation in his throat from the tube that had kept him alive for more than 24 hours.

After dressing, Dan checked the time, seeing he still had five minutes before the 10 am meeting. This call had been scheduled for 8 am but had been pushed back last minute. Dan hoped that wasn't done to allow him more time to sleep. Now he headed to the basement stairs and slowly descended. He took extra care in light of what he'd been through but found the stairs were no more challenging than before the attack.

Entering the family room, he went to the desk and

powered up the computer. He then adjusted the camera and volume and clicked on the link Mac had sent to his email.

Seconds later, he saw the conference room at the Midtown Detective Bureau and the newly formed task force members.

"Dan. Nice of you to join us!" Tom Koster said.

"It's great to see you looking good, Dan. When will you be back to work?" Detective Jenny Moore asked.

Like Dan, she wasn't present in the room. She connected with her laptop from a small sheriff's office in Montana.

"I'll be there before the end of the week. I'm feeling 99 percent now and am just waiting to get cleared."

After a few more questions about Dan's health, Mac said, "Okay, let's get going. We'll report on what we have been learning. But first, this meeting had to be delayed this morning because he struck again."

"What happened?" Dan asked with concern in his voice.

"It was another failure," Tom said with an odd smirk that seemed out of place to Dan.

Mac nodded in agreement. "This guy is either a dangerous idiot or highly accident-prone. Those of us here all made it to the scene and interviewed the intended victim, who never even saw the guy. He'd already gone when she got home after taking her morning walk.

"He broke in through a bedroom window, made it 10 feet, and encountered a 200-pound English mastiff. Our guy fired the Taser at the dog and missed as he scurried back out the window. We found some blood but aren't sure if the broken window caused it or if the dog got him."

"Are you sure it was our guy and not a burglar?" Dan asked.

"Certain. The serial numbers on the Taser AFIDs match the stolen batch," Mac explained.

"That doesn't make sense," Dan added. "We were sure he carefully scopes out the houses he plans to hit. It would be impossible to miss a mastiff living there."

Laughing, Lieutenant Miller added, "That's the best part."

"What do you mean?" Jenny Moore asked.

Mac continued with the story, "The dog doesn't live there. The intended victim agreed to dog-sit for her sister. The dog arrived less than 12 hours before our friend broke in. Probably well after the assailant would have picked the house as a target."

This generated laughter from those who hadn't been on the scene.

"Well, if the dog wasn't a welcome house guest before, I'm sure he is now," Dan commented.

"Okay. Let's review what we have learned. Jenny, you start," Mac instructed.

"I met with the rancher. The incident was so bizarre he remembers the details well. Besides what we already know, the rancher found a can of FoamX lying by one of the cows. Also, there was a third cow attacked."

This news got everyone's attention.

"Same ranch?" Dan asked.

"No. That's where it gets interesting. It happened a week before the other cows were killed and on a neighboring property. They found a cow wandering the field with half its nose full of foam. The local sheriff believes, and I agree, that this was his first attempt, and the assailant either tried to hold the cow with a rope or it was loose and pulled away when the foam was applied.

"We think our guy changed locations because there are no trees on this first property. He could better secure the animals to the tree at the site where he succeeded."

"Did the first cow survive?" Tom asked.

"Yeah, it sounds like the cow pulled away immediately. One side of its nose had foam filling it, but nothing more. A vet came in and dug the foam out after sedating the cow. We think that's why he changed to securing them to trees."

Lieutenant Miller asked, "Were there any fingerprints on the spray cans?"

"I looked into prints, and the sheriff's office did check for them at the time, and there were none on the can," Detective Moore confirmed.

"How about a lot number from the recovered can? I'm running that angle, and it could help," Detective Jenkins asked.

"Not sure. I'll check as soon as I get off the call. I've seen the report but not the actual can. I don't know if they kept it or recorded the lot number," Jenny Moore explained.

After a few seconds to process the information, Mac said, "That's good. Anything else?"

"I've been showing the sketch around, and all law enforcement agencies in the state have a copy. One person at the ranch where the attack failed thinks the guy looked familiar but couldn't place him. No one else has recognized him. I fly back tomorrow and will be showing the picture around a bit more before I leave. That's all I have."

"Thanks, Jenny. Let us know if you learn anything more. George, what've you found?" Mac said.

Detective George Jenkins nodded and said, "I've been running with the lot numbers on the FoamX can. The manufacturer is cooperative, and I found the lot number was assigned to a group of a thousand cans. All were sent to a large online retailer. I contacted them, and they told me the lot became split between three of their distribution centers. One of which is here in Arizona. Last night, I sent them a court order to release customer information, and they agreed to have it for me later today. That should tell us where all the cans in the lot ended up. I'll focus on the ones shipped to the local distribution center first, focusing on sales of multiple cans together. Going through all that data may take a day or two."

"Sounds good. Tom, did you learn anything about the attack at the veterinary office?"

"The victim's name was Diego Garcia. He was one of four vets in the practice. He was the on-call vet that weekend and had recently handled an emergency call on Sunday. He either never left or came back. The location and method of attack seem off, and we know our subject was wounded in an attack Sunday morning. The timing fits. So I believe he went to the veterinary office for medical care. Then killed the vet that treated him."

Everyone thought about what was said, then Jenny asked, "But why that vet? It was an hour away. There are many much closer."

Mac agreed. "Keep digging, Tom," she said. "There's something more there."

"Will do."

"Thanks. I'm following up on the rubber-glove fragment," Mac said. "The lab report shows the fragment is from a nitrile rubber glove. Apparently, there are hundreds of brands of gloves on the market. This one was made by a company called Planet One Industries. They sell the same gloves under the names Tough Finger and Fine Touch. They're non-surgical, medical exam gloves. None of the major hospitals in the area use these brands. Planet One is complying with the court order and getting me a list of local customers. Still, these gloves are also available online, and anyone can order a box. There will be thousands of businesses and individuals to sort through."

Chapter 37

Since disconnecting from the conference call, Detective Jenny Moore had been busy. She'd checked on the spray foam can used in the attack on the cows. The lot number hadn't been recorded, and the can was no longer available to check. It had either been lost or discarded in the past three years.

There were three other ranches in the area, and she had visited two of them, showing the sketch with no results.

Her flight home would leave in the morning, so she headed to visit one last ranch before it got too late. The drive took almost two hours, and when she arrived, she saw that the property was immense, going on for many miles. She entered the main drive and past numerous buildings before arriving at the main house.

As she approached, a man in his mid-fifties was coming outside. He stood slightly over average height and wore a cowboy hat, denim shirt, and jeans.

Giving her a curious look, he said, "Ma'am, what can I do for you?"

"I'm looking for the owner of the property," Jenny said.

"He isn't here and won't be back for a couple of days. I'm

Mike, and I'm in charge when he isn't around. What do you need?"

Displaying her credentials, she said, "I'm with the Tucson Police Department and would like to talk to some of your people."

"Tucson, Arizona? I think you might be a bit lost," Mike chuckled.

Jenny smiled briefly, then replied, "We have a serial killer in Tucson, and there's a connection to two ranches in this area from a few years back. I want to show a sketch to your workers and see if they recognize him."

"Let me see it."

The detective opened the folder and took a copy of the sketch she'd printed off at the local sheriff's office. She handed the sheet of paper to the ranch foreman, who scrutinized it before saying, "I've seen this guy. I'm not sure where, but I'm pretty sure I've seen him."

Jenny felt her heart rate increase.

Without handing the page back, Mike said, "Follow me, Detective. Most of the guys live on-site here and are having supper down at the bunkhouse. Let's see if any of them remember him."

They got in a tan pickup truck with the ranch logo on the door and drove several minutes to a long, single-story building. Almost a dozen men were outside standing around a hot grill talking; most were holding bottles of beer in their hands.

As they climbed out of the truck, Mike called out, "Get everyone out here."

Jenny and Mike walked over as more men came out of the building.

"This is Police Detective Moore. She came all the way from Arizona to talk to you. Be courteous," Mike told the assembled group.

The men became quiet, and Jenny took out several more copies of the sketch and handed them out. "I need to know if any of you recognize this man," she began. "He would have been in the area a few years back."

The men passed the sheets around and then started whispering to one another. Some shrugged, but others were more engaged.

Finally, one of the ranch hands spoke. "I remember him," he confirmed. "He came here with the students from the veterinary college a few years back."

"Yea, that's right. He was here a few times," another said.

More men agreed, and Jenny asked, "Does anyone remember his name?"

They all shook their heads.

Mike explained, "We work with the veterinary college in Billings. Several times a year, they send students here. Normally we do all our own immunizations of the herds. However, sometimes the students come on-site to get some experience, which takes work off our plates. Later in their training, as veterinary residents, they'll come here occasionally and help with more extensive care. We have a good working relationship with the school."

Nodding, Jenny asked, "Is there anything else anyone remembers about this guy?"

The gathered ranch hands either shook their heads or verbally apologized.

"Well, that's a big help. It gets me a step closer. Thanks for your time."

As they left, Jenny asked Mike, "How long a drive is it to the veterinary school?"

"About two hours."

Jenny looked at the time on her phone, and her stomach sank. It was after six in the evening. There'd be no trip home in the morning.

Chapter 38

That night, Jenny Moore changed her flight until late the next day and called Mac to update her on the investigation. They now understood why the killer felt comfortable with larger animals.

The following morning, she checked out of the hotel, hoping the departure wasn't premature, and headed to the veterinary college in Billings. It was, as Mike had said, almost a two-hour drive, and she passed the time listening to a podcast saved on her phone.

Arriving at the campus, she found her way to the veterinary sciences building and went inside. The administration office was off to the left, and she headed there and stepped inside.

A woman in her late twenties looked up as Jenny approached and said, "Good morning. What can I do for you?" Her name tag read Lucy.

Jenny displayed her credentials, "I'm here as part of a homicide investigation. I need to talk to someone about a former student."

"What's the student's name?"

"I don't know. I have a sketch and need to see if any of the faculty recognizes it."

"Can I see it?" Lucy asked.

Jenny handed it over, and the woman scrutinized it, "Do you know how long ago he was a student here?"

"We believe it would've been about two or three years ago."

"That would've been before my time, and my co-worker is out today. Doctor Chandler has been in charge of the program for a long time and knows all the students. He's in class now, but I can send him a message to come up here as soon as the class period is over. It should only be about 10 minutes or so."

Jenny took a seat, trying not to fidget as she impatiently waited. After more than 15 minutes, the office door opened, and a stocky man in his early sixties entered the room. He talked briefly to Lucy and then approached Jenny.

"Detective? I'm Doctor Walter Chandler. I'm the director of the School of Veterinary Sciences."

Jenny stood and shook his hand.

"Thank you for meeting me. I need to show you a sketch and see if you recognize it. I suspect he might have been a student here."

She handed the sketch over and watched as recognition flashed on the professor's face.

"May I ask what you believe he did?" The man said.

"We want to speak to him about several murders that happened in Tucson."

"That's interesting. This sketch looks a lot like Evan Brown. He studied here several years ago."

After a pause, Doctor Chandler added, "Let's go to my office and discuss Evan," he suggested.

They turned and went a short distance and entered a small office. They sat together at a table, and Doctor Chandler brought up his former student's file on his laptop. The information was displayed on a wall-mounted screen where Jenny could see it.

The first thing they viewed was a student photo that looked a lot like the sketch.

"Evan was here for a year and a half before I convinced him to leave," Doctor Chandler explained.

"Why did you want him to leave? Poor academics?" Jenny asked.

"He was a bit of an outcast and never mixed well with the other students, but his test scores were excellent. The problem was how he related to animals. A veterinarian needs to care genuinely about animals, and it became apparent he didn't. He saw them as an inconvenience. After hearing some complaints, I watched how he acted, and he had no compassion. Evan did what he was supposed to do to care for them, and he was never cruel but he clearly had no genuine interest in them.

"Eventually, he and I had a few conversations. In the end, I suggested that animal care wasn't for him. Shortly after the discussion, he withdrew from school, and I never saw him again."

"Any idea why he enrolled in vet school if he didn't care about animals?" Jenny asked.

The professor nodded and said, "He and I discussed it. Apparently, he had a younger sister whom he was very close to. She always wanted to be a veterinarian but died at a young age. He thought becoming a vet would make him feel closer to her."

"Do you have a record of any family or emergency contacts?"

The professor searched the online record and shook his head. "None were ever listed. If I remember, they were all deceased."

"What about friends? Were there any other students he was close to?"

Professor Chandler thought for a few seconds. "Evan was a loner, but there was one student he seemed close to. His name is Diego Garcia."

Jenny's jaw dropped, and her eyes went wide.

"I take it that name is familiar to you?"

"Yeah, that name has come up in our investigation," Jenny said.

After a few additional questions, Jenny was given an electronic copy of Evan's school records and his photo, which she'd forward to Mac.

She'd hit paydirt and now could head to the airport and home.

Chapter 39

Dan Felty sat in a recliner in his living room. It was 9 am on a Thursday, and the boredom was extreme. The kids were at school, and his wife had gone back to work. He'd already taken the dogs for a long walk, and now he sat feeling useless.

He was looking forward to the next day. The doctors had told him he could return to work on Friday if he felt up to it. But for now, he sat looking at all the terrible options on the TV before turning it off for the second time this morning.

His ringing phone startled him. He was glad for the distraction but recognized the ringtone as Mac's, and he assumed she was calling only to check up on him again.

"Yes, Mac. I'm still feeling fine," he said immediately.

"Good. I'm glad to hear it. It'll be good to have you back tomorrow," she said. The fatigue was evident in her voice.

"Are you okay?" Dan asked. "You sound exhausted."

"I'm a bit tired," she admitted. "Last night, I got the customer data from Planet One right before I headed home. It has all the sales of their gloves in the area. I woke up at two in the morning and couldn't sleep thinking about it, so I came in and have been poring over it, making a list of the purchasers to check on. I've already visited a couple of clinics in the area; all were dead ends."

"Anything I can do?"

"Well, you aren't supposed to be working yet, but you live only a few miles from the city animal shelter. They happen to buy a couple of hundred boxes of Tough Finger gloves each year. I'll need to send someone from the task force over to show the sketch around."

"I've been considering taking a drive and could easily pass by there," Dan said eagerly. It was a simple task, but he'd welcome the chance to do something productive.

Disconnecting the call, he thought for a minute, knowing he shouldn't be working. Still, unable to help himself, he went to his nightstand and took his badge and gun from the drawer. He'd have to make sure not to tell Abby about this errand. If she found out Mac gave him a task when he should still be resting, the women's relationship might return to where it was before he'd been drugged.

Getting in his car, Dan drove the six miles to the Tucson Animal Shelter, enjoying the feeling of being out of the house. He parked by the main entrance and headed inside. An older couple stood ahead of him at the counter, talking to an employee about adopting a senior dog.

A young female employee saw Dan and approached, giving him a confused look. "Can I help you with something?" she asked.

Showing her his badge, he said, "I'm with the police and need to speak to whoever's in charge."

The woman's face changed with recognition. "I knew you looked familiar. You're the detective attacked at the police station. Your face is on all the news sites."

Nodding, Dan said. "That's me. But I'm back at work now."

"I'm so glad. The stories made it sound terrible."

Dan smiled and nodded, not wanting to discuss the details with someone he didn't know. "It was."

"Please wait here, detective. I'll go and get my boss."

After a brief wait, another woman approached and spoke to Dan, "I'm Amber Goddard, the facility manager. Do we need to talk in private?"

"I'm not sure yet," Dan answered as he handed his phone to the woman. She looked at the photo of the sketch of the attacker on the screen.

Watching Amber's face, he felt his heart rate increase as soon as she looked at the image; the recognition was obvious.

"That's Evan Brown. He's an employee here."

Barely able to control his excitement, Dan responded, "Is he here now?"

"No, he usually works later in the afternoons, but today's his day off," Amber explained.

"Okay, now we need to talk in private, and please get his personal file. Do you have a cell number for him?" Dan asked, hoping they could track Evan's phone.

"No, he never gave us a cell number. Only his house phone."

Amber led him to a private room that they used to interview potential adopters. Dan took his phone back, closed the photo, opened the text messaging app, and selected Mac's name.

"JACKPOT. Name is Evan Brown. He works at the animal shelter but is off today. About to review his file and get a photo and address. Will call soon."

He hit the send button, and the message was on Mac's phone in a few seconds.

MAC WAS IN SHOCK WHEN SEEING THE NAME. THE SAME NAME had appeared on her screen two minutes earlier, sent from Montana.

Chapter 40

THE CONFERENCE ROOM THAT THE TASK FORCE HAD TAKEN over had a whole new feel now that they had a name and address. All the team members were digging into who Evan Brown was.

Earlier that morning, the listing of all the FoamX cans sold from the local distribution center came in. While waiting for the meeting to start, detective Jenkins scanned the list.

"Hey, Mac," he called out. "This is the list of FoamX sales from the local distribution center. There's an Evan Brown listed as a purchaser. He ordered 12 cans about six weeks ago."

"More confirmation," Mac said. "Good work. Everything is starting to come together."

The team fidgeted restlessly. They had Evan's name and address and now awaited news that the search warrant for his property had been issued.

Evan lived outside the city limits, so the task force needed to coordinate their efforts with the Pima County Sheriff's Department. Having one of their members on the team now proved invaluable.

Lieutenant Miller walked into the room and spotted Dan Felty sitting at a table working on a laptop.

"Felty, you're still on medical leave. You aren't supposed to be working until tomorrow."

"I'm just visiting with my co-workers, LT."

"Really? You expect me to believe that."

Dan smiled.

Resigned, Miller said, "When we raid the property, you aren't going. That better be clear."

Visibly disappointed with the order, Dan reluctantly agreed.

Addressing the room, the lieutenant said, "Listen up. There's another development. We have a video call with an agent of the US Marshals Service."

"Marshals? What do they want? Is our guy a fugitive?" Mac asked.

"No idea. I got a call from the chief of detectives, saying they wanted to talk to us. The call is in three minutes."

The screen on the wall lit up as Mac activated the video conference, and soon a middle-aged woman appeared on the screen.

"Good morning. I'm Tanya Cole with the US Marshals Service."

"I'm Lieutenant Miller with the Tucson Detective Bureau. This is Mackenzie Bell, the task force leader, and the rest of her team is here too."

"I understand your department is looking into Evan Brown," Marshal Cole said.

"We are. How do you know about him?" Mac asked. "We learned his name only a few hours ago."

"Years back, Mr. Brown was under the protection of the Marshals Service. While we no longer actively offer him protection, we still keep a watch on all governmental databases in case a former protectee's name comes up. It's still possible certain people could come looking for him. What's it you're investigating him for?"

"Serial homicide. We have a dozen bodies and strong evidence he's responsible," Mac explained.

On the screen, Tanya cursed. "I hoped this would be something we could clear up quietly, but that obviously isn't going to be possible," she said.

"What can you tell us about Evan? You clearly know more about him than we do," Mac asked.

"Normally, we would never share the background of someone under our protection, but Evan is no longer in the program. His mother voluntarily left the program shortly after first being relocated."

"But you still keep an eye on him? You quickly knew we were looking into him," Dan asked.

"Once under our protection, we watch out for anyone looking into them, even if they choose to leave. This will be a long story," Tanya explained.

"We have time," Mac said.

Chapter 41

15 YEARS EARLIER

BRIAN CONNOR LEFT THE LARGE OFFICE BUILDING ON THE outskirts of Chicago. His eyes were red, and tears flowed down his cheeks as he moved slowly along. His stomach churned, and he'd vomited several minutes before in the men's room at his attorney's office.

Even though tomorrow he'd surrender himself to federal agents and head to prison, today was the worst day of his life. In about an hour, he'd be telling his family the news. His wife already knew most of it, but the children didn't, and he wasn't sure how to tell them. They were so young they probably couldn't even understand. They'd only know their dad would be leaving.

He crossed the street to the parking garage and took the stairs to the top level. Brian walked to the rail at the edge and looked down at the street below. The idea tempted him. This nightmare could all be over in a few seconds. No prison and no seeing the looks on his kid's faces when he told them they'd never see him again.

But he couldn't do that. He loved them too much not to say goodbye. He couldn't go, letting them think he wanted to be gone from their lives. He needed to tell his children this was his fault and not theirs.

He and his nine-year-old son Blake had a fantastic relationship and did everything they could together. Picturing the damage this would do to his boy crushed Brian's heart.

After several minutes he stepped back from the rail and took the stairs down to the fourth level. Finding his six-month-old BMW Sports Coupe, he got in and started the engine. He loved this car, and today would be his last time driving it. Sadly he realized he might never drive anything again. That's what happens when you kill a federal agent, even accidentally.

His arrest hadn't been a surprise. He'd always expected it might happen, and he thought he was prepared to manage it. He planned to testify and provide extremely valuable information in exchange for protection if arrested. He'd get to remain with his family. They'd be relocated with new names, and he had several million dollars stashed in an offshore account that the government would never know about. He had a solid plan until he panicked and made the biggest mistake of his life.

He left the garage and headed home and, for the thousandth time, thought about the day everything went wrong, and the tears returned.

On that fateful day, four weeks ago, he'd been working in the small office he rented.

He was transferring large amounts of electronic funds between various offshore shell companies.

His job involved taking the millions of dollars in cash he received each week and cleaning it through a series of semi-legitimate businesses he managed. He then transferred the deposited funds out of the United States, where they went into other businesses which his employers in South America controlled.

Brian never asked where the money came from and could therefore pretend he wasn't doing anything wrong. Still, whenever he read about an illegal drug seizure, the back of his brain knew.

He'd never find out who it was, but someone in the organization had been arrested. They gave Brian and his money laundering operation up to the authorities in exchange for a deal.

He was so careful with what he did that no one would have figured out his involvement otherwise.

While in the restroom that fateful day, he heard a crashing sound and muted yelling and rushed back to his office. The previously locked door now stood ajar, and four men in windbreakers, the letters FBI on the back, were inside.

Brian had a big problem. He hadn't secured the computers, and all the data they contained was accessible. If the agents confiscated the data, he'd lose his value as an informant, and his carefully crafted plans might fall apart.

He sprinted into the room and raced to the side of the desk where there were two large buttons.

A male agent who looked to be in his mid-thirties stepped in front of him, and Brian dropped his shoulder and powered into the man who fell back. In the corner of the room sat a three-foot square steel cage containing the servers and all the data. The agent crashed into it, striking the back of his head.

Brian pressed the two buttons, and the large electromagnets inside the cage charged and created an intense magnetic field that destroyed most of the computer data. At the same time, electrical capacitors in the cage charged and then released a powerful burst of electromagnetic energy, further destroying the sensitive equipment.

The agents wrestled Brian to the ground and handcuffed him as he exhaled with relief. He was now in a position to make a good deal with the authorities in exchange for his testimony. Then something caught his eye. At the steel server cage, the agent who'd tried to stop him lay still on the ground, not moving, and a growing pool of blood was coming from the back of his head.

Brian later learned the agent who died that day had also been the father of young children. The opportunity for him to walk away from this with a new life died at the moment the agent had.

His attention snapped back to his driving, knowing what happened would continue to replay in his head for as long as he lived.

Turning on to his street, Brian looked at the neighborhood as he drove slowly along, delaying the inevitable.

Turning into the drive, he stopped in front of the three-car garage and sat viewing the beautiful home he and his wife Judy had grown to love.

She'd be devastated to learn that she'd have to give up the home and lifestyle she loved so much and Brian now had to tell her.

He entered the house and heard the kids in the backyard. He walked to the slider and saw the children in the pool with their diligent mother watching over them.

He was so proud of his children. This was the first year Cindy would get in the pool. Her fear of the water and drowning had kept her out until now. Blake had been an enormous part of her success as he patiently worked with her, showing her that it was safe to put her face in the water as he held her.

The young girl loved and trusted her big brother in everything they did.

He slid the patio door open and walked out. Judy heard it and ran to him and held him as he wept.

"There's an agreement?" she asked.

"Yes. I have to be at the federal building at 10 tomorrow morning."

"And no trial?"

"No trial. I plead guilty and tell the feds everything, and you and the kids will be relocated and protected."

"I don't want to be relocated! I like my life. I like my home and my friends!" Judy screamed.

"I know. But the South Americans will come after you to punish me."

"South Americans!" she echoed. "Stop calling them that! The term is a drug cartel. That's who you work for. A drug cartel!"

Brian didn't say anything.

Hearing the commotion, the kids looked up.

"Daddy's home!" nine-year-old Blake yelled.

He and his six-year-old sister Cindy got out of the pool and ran to the father they adored. Brian bent down and clutched the wet children, treasuring the moment.

Hours later, he lay in bed thinking about his conversation with them after dinner. He knew the sounds of their weeping would never leave his memory. But what was worse were the words Blake said over and over through his tears, "I love you, daddy. Please don't leave us."

Chapter 42

THE TASK FORCE MEMBERS LISTENED AS TANYA EXPLAINED HOW the marshal's office knew about Evan Brown.

"So I assume that means young Blake Connor became Evan Brown when you relocated him?" Mac asked.

"Correct," Tanya confirmed. "The Connors were relocated from Chicago to Montana. They were provided with a small home, and Judy, who now went by the name Sue Brown, worked in a chain department store. They were safe from those who wanted to punish Brian, but things got worse for them."

"What's that mean?" Detective Koster asked.

"Sue Brown didn't adjust well to the change. She missed the luxuries that were now gone from her life and strongly resented the situation. She started drinking a lot. After a couple of years, she married a man named Ray Williams. From what we could tell, Ray tried to be a good stepfather but couldn't compare to Brian as a husband, father, or provider, and Sue's drinking got worse.

"It didn't help that Ray drank, too, and the two of them fought a lot. There's no indication he ever hurt the kids. Evan and his sister Patti, formerly Cindy, became very close during this time. When Evan was 11 and Patti 8, the family was in a car accident. Evan was thrown from the wreck, but the vehicle went into a lake, and the other three didn't get out. Evan watched the vehicle sink, knowing they were drowning and unable to do anything because of his injuries."

"They drowned?" Mac said.

"Yes, Evan fell apart after that. He'd adored and watched over his sister and blamed himself for being unable to save her," the marshal explained.

"That's huge information," Mac said. "Evan is killing with a type of controlled drowning."

"That makes sense. He ended up in several foster homes. One of them had him removed after they realized he'd drowned several neighborhood animals."

"I guess that fits with his background and what he's doing now," Dan commented.

"What else can you tell us?" Mac asked.

"Not much. He's stayed off our radar since the animal-killing incident. We haven't had any reason to look into him," Tanya explained.

"Is Evan's father still in prison?" Detective Koster asked.

"He is. He failed to make parole several years ago, but he'll be eligible again in a few more months."

"Do he and Evan have any contact?" Detective Jenkins asked.

"No. The protection agreement ensured there'd be no contact. I doubt Evan's father even knows his ex-wife and daughter are dead," the marshal explained.

Chapter 43

Mackenzie Bell sat in the driver's seat of her department-issued SUV with Lieutenant Miller next to her. They both wore tactical ballistic vests and felt their elevated heart rates while waiting for the other task force members to join up.

After a couple of minutes, the radio alerted her that the other officers were in position.

"This is Bell. Everyone move in!" she said into the microphone on her shoulder.

Three vehicles approached the house from different directions. Two on the street and a third racing across the empty dirt lot at the back of the house.

As they arrived, they noticed that there were no vehicles there. The house was small and tan with faded trim. The whole thing badly needed new paint. The yard was dirt with a single small cactus for vegetation. There were no fences on the property line, and the trash can against the house was overflowing.

Mac cringed, knowing that everything in the trash can would need to be searched through by hand over the next couple of days.

Screeching to a halt, four task force members exited their vehicles and raced to the front door. Mac pounded on it and yelled, "Evan Brown, this is the Tucson police. We have a search warrant. No one opened the door from the inside, so a battering ram struck the door adjacent to the deadbolt, blasting it inward.

Mac went through the doorway first with her gun up and sweeping left to right. She heard the back door crashing open as she moved through the living room. In seconds her people had verified that Evan wasn't home and began searching the house.

Despite the desert air, the home smelled musty with a slight scent of decay. There was a pile of unwashed dishes in the sink, and a pot with old dried-out pasta sat on the stove.

The bathroom wasn't filthy, but no one had cleaned it for a long time, and the trash can overflowed with bloody bandages.

On the bedroom room wall were a dozen framed photos. All contained a pre-teen girl. The photos spanned several years as her features looked different in each. A few also contained a woman who Mac assumed was Evan's mother. In some cases, one of two men accompanied her. One of which the detective recognized from the image the marshal had shown them of Evan's father.

A young Evan appeared in some of the group photos. The photos were arranged so that they surrounded two large blown-up images of only the girl. The large ones reminded Mac of the kind of photos that kids had taken at school.

Mac moved to a back bedroom that had been converted into a workroom to start her search. Old storage cabinets were mounted on the wall, and a folding table sat below. On the table was a cardboard box containing unused Taser cartridges but no Taser gun.

Discarded on the floor, in the corner, she spotted a white metal box. It had brackets for mounting to a wall, which were bent and damaged. Turning it over, she saw the familiar logo for Wildwood Veterinary Services with the words "Controlled Substances" under it.

The box was empty except for a broken padlock that someone had cut with bolt cutters.

Returning her attention to the wall-mounted cabinets, she opened the one on the left and saw four unopened cans of FoamX. On the right were several glass vials of injectable medications and a tranquilizer pistol.

With a gloved hand, she removed a larger vial and read the word ketamine on the label.

Now that the house appeared safe, an evidence technician had arrived and started photographing everything.

"Hey, Mac. Check this out," Detective Jenkins said.

She walked over and saw him looking and a matchbox-size wireless camera. A green LED glowed brightly on the front.

"Is it on?" Mac asked.

"Looks like it. Evan might be watching us now."

Mac picked it up and pressed the power button on the back. The LED stopped glowing.

She pressed the microphone on her shoulder. "We found a small camera watching us," she reported. "There might be more. Shut them off if you find them."

Tom Koster's voice followed hers, "There is a wireless motion sensor by the back door. Check the front."

Seconds later, one of the other sheriff's deputies replied, "There's one at the front, too. I suspect our subject knew we were here as soon as we entered."

Mac cursed, knowing that Evan wouldn't be returning. She called out, "No reason to be neat. He won't be coming back. Take this place apart. Let's find everything we can."

Chapter 44

Evan Brown sat on the concrete patio of his latest victim, crying and shaking from the torment that haunted him. He thought about his failure to protect his sister and what she'd endured in her final minutes. Years ago, she'd fought for breath, as the woman on the ground in front of him had done seconds ago. All the time he spent teaching Patti to swim and not to be afraid of drowning had been in vain. In the end, she had been right to be scared. Drowning would eventually get her.

He glanced at the woman on her back with solidified foam protruding from her mouth and nose and wondered what Patti would have been like if she had lived to be this woman's age. Evan felt sure she'd be finishing veterinary school, or maybe she'd be married and have several children of her own. Understanding that these opportunities had been robbed from her brought a new wave of tears.

A full 10 minutes after his victim's heart had stopped, Evan had composed himself enough to leave.

As he shoved the expended Taser cartridge and half-full FoamX can into his backpack, his phone chirped with a tone he'd seldom heard.

He glanced at the screen and his breath caught when he saw an alert that said, *"Motion detected. Sensor 1 activated."*

As he pondered the message, another came in, *"Motion detected. Sensor 4 activated."*

Understanding what this meant, he launched the app that connected to the hidden cameras placed throughout his house.

On the screen, he began scrolling through the cameras but was briefly interrupted when Sensor 3 alerted him.

He watched as heavily armed people swarmed through the rooms of his house with their weapons raised.

The quality of the video wasn't the best, but he recognized the short female detective who'd shot at him as she chased him down the alley.

He wanted to flee but couldn't stop watching as his privacy was violated on the screen. He shook with rage as they opened the cabinets in his workroom, and photos were taken of the contents.

Evan struggled to comprehend how they'd found him. He'd been careful and hadn't suspected that they'd been close to identifying him.

As he watched, an unfamiliar man noticed the tiny camera in the workroom. His face got close as he examined it.

Evan could see him call out to someone, and then the short woman approached and also looked at the camera. The image jolted violently as the camera moved and then went dark. Over the next three minutes, Evan watched as the other cameras were all found and stopped transmitting, one at a time.

Chapter 45

A LESS-THAN-ENTHUSIASTIC TEAM GATHERED IN AN UNUSED section of the Pima County Sheriff's fleet building the following morning. Six eight-foot-long folding tables were pushed together to make a large work surface. It was two tables wide and three long. A large blue vinyl tarp covered the assembly.

Evidence technicians from the city police and the sheriff's department worked together, dumping out the bags of garbage collected from Evan Brown's home, one at a time. They spread the contents across the tarp, looking for useful evidence.

Unimpressed with the assignment he'd been given on his first day back to work, Dan Felty stood back, overseeing the operation. As the evidence technicians searched, he was available in case they discovered anything of interest.

All those involved in the work wore rubber gloves, white disposable full-body suits, and a medical-grade face mask. Inside each mask, the wearer had smeared a dab of mentholated ointment of the kind that would typically be rubbed on the chest of a sick child to help with coughing. In this case, the strong menthol smell protected them from the wretched stench of the rotting garbage, some of which had been sitting outside Evan's house in the 90-degree temperatures for several weeks.

When they dumped the first bag, they all groaned as the foul waste landed on the table, followed by grey liquid that had pooled at the bottom of the bag.

The army of evidence technicians spread the contents across the tables, then attacked the pile. One woman was taking photos, thankful her superior had assigned her the camera. The other six people began sorting. The team gathered up uneaten food waste and threw it in a disposal barrel. Food wrappers and any packing material were quickly searched in case Evan had written notes on them and then disposed of, too.

Anything with blood on it was placed in a tote, where it would undergo further photography and testing to confirm that the blood came from Evan.

They examined the rest in closer detail. Every item was checked to determine if it should be kept and tested further. So far, those items had been few and included two used darts and four expended Taser cartridges. Almost everything else held no interest to the investigators, who continued to look for something of value.

"Detective," one of the technicians called out.

Dan walked over and received a page torn from a spiral notebook. It had a list of addresses on it. Some had lines through them, and others had a checkmark next to them. Dan recognized the ones that had a check mark. Those were all addresses where Evan had attempted an attack. The list ran to the bottom of the page.

The woman took a photo of the page and then placed it in a sealed evidence-collection bag.

Dan suspected there was a second page to the list still in

the notebook and walked a few steps away so his conversation wouldn't interrupt those working.

Removing his gloves, he worked his hand under the protective gown and withdrew his phone.

Mac answered on the second ring. "Hey, Dan. Did you find anything?"

"We aren't even halfway done, but I found what looks like a target list. Did you guys recover a spiral-bound notebook?"

"We have two. I found one with his veterinary texts, and it's full of school notes, nothing else. The other looked to be new. There were no pages ripped out and no imprints from writing on any pages."

"It sounds like there's a third notebook, and he has it with him. I have a long list of potential target addresses on the page. It runs the full length of the sheet. Some are checked off, and the others are crossed out. The last two victims aren't on the list, so I think there's another page of addresses still in the book," Dan explained.

"Are there names too, or only addresses?"

"Just addresses. I doubt he knows or cares who they are," Dan said.

"I'll have someone look into the crossed-out addresses, if we can make them out. If we find out why Evan crossed them off, we might be able to better understand why he chooses the people he does," Mac said.

"I'll send you a photo of the page as soon as we hang up."

As they spoke, an evidence technician approached. Even with her mask on, Dan could read her excitement by her body language.

"Hold on, Mac."

Dan took the phone away from his face and said, "Find something?"

"Sure did. A cell phone bill."

She handed over another evidence bag containing a single

sheet of paper. The page had wrinkles and stains from liquids. Looking at it, Dan saw a current cell phone bill, and despite the damage to the page, the account number and phone number were clear.

Chapter 46

Evan paced back and forth in the isolated dirt parking lot like a lion in a cage. His throat felt raw from screaming at himself for his failure. The police had invaded his privacy, and his fury burned. Being denied access to his belongings made it all worse.

Evan walked from one end of the parking lot to the other and back again. As he did, he watched, for the 12th time, the video that the cameras had saved to their supplier's online cloud site. Each time he watched it, he felt his rage grow. He'd put so much hard work and risk into obtaining his equipment, and it was now all lost. Access to all his other belongings was gone, too, including all the photos of Patti. Fortunately, he had copies of most of them online and could view them on his phone or tablet.

Forcing himself to relax, he pushed the rage away. He needed to think clearly. He'd known something like this would eventually happen, and he even had some plans for when it did. But all the preparation faded from his mind when he saw the police searching his home. Now he needed to pull himself together and put a plan in place.

His Taser pistol held two cartridges, and he'd used only

one on his last attack, and the FoamX can he used was still half full. Smiling, Evan decided he'd find one more target, if for no other reason than to show the short detective that she hadn't stopped him. But before that, he had something else he needed to do. He had to go back to his house one last time.

Returning to his car, he looked around to make sure no one was watching, then retrieved a screwdriver from the back-seat floor and removed his license plate. He then went to one of the other vehicles in the lot and swapped his plate for theirs.

He knew this would be of limited value, but he only needed it to help protect him for another hour or so. Then he'd abandon the car.

He drove to a local thrift store that would soon be closing for the night. He went in, and searched for several minutes, finally finding a small tan duffle bag. Taking it, he went to the men's clothing section and, without looking at sizes, selected a sweatshirt with no concern about style or color. Purchasing the items with cash, he returned to his car.

He drove eight miles across town and headed out into the desert, stopping at a small commuter parking lot. Evan was aware of a seldom-used trail at the back of the lot. He'd hiked it before and knew it would take him within a half-mile of his home. Gathering up the duffel bag and his backpack, he set off along the trail into the setting sun.

An hour later, the growing darkness was making it difficult to see. Still, he recognized the landmarks and left the trail, walking another 15 minutes until he saw the back of his house.

He desperately wanted to go inside and see what remained of his home but knew the police might still be watching the house from the road.

He slowly approached the small aging utility shed in the backyard and opened the door. The police had searched the shed, too, because nothing was where it belonged.

Finding the long-handled shovel against the wall, he took it and returned to the desert.

Near the edge of his property, there were two cacti, each about four feet high and 20 feet apart. He lined himself up between them and walked until he stood about an equal distance between each. Looking at the ground, Evan spotted a flat stone that'd look completely natural to anyone else. He kicked it aside and started digging where it had been.

The sand and stones were loose enough to make the digging easy. When he'd removed about eight inches of dirt, the shovel struck something solid, and the killer smiled.

It took only another minute to uncover the three-foot-long section of four-inch-diameter PVC pipe. Typically used for sewer lines, the small section had a solid cap glued on one end and a screw cap on the other to protect the valuable contents from any rain or creatures.

Evan strained but eventually unscrewed the cap he'd put on more than six months before.

Using the moonlight, he withdrew the contents. First, there were a thousand dollars in $20 bills, followed by two prepaid debit cards. Lastly, he withdrew a large zipped plastic bag containing a single document. Evan took it out and checked to ensure it wasn't damaged.

It was a birth certificate with the name Blake Connor on it. He'd come into the world as Blake, and now he'd start using his real name again.

Chapter 47

Amber Goddard drove her small red Honda SUV into the parking lot and stopped in her usual spot. On her way to work, she'd stopped at a bagel shop and picked up a breakfast sandwich with sausage, egg, and cheese. She got out of the vehicle carrying her backpack over her shoulder. She headed to the rear employee door with her breakfast in hand. She swiped her badge, and the door released, allowing her access to the Tucson Animal Shelter.

As she did, she remembered something she'd meant to do the previous day but had forgotten. Amber needed to send a message to the City Services Department and have Evan Brown's employee access terminated. She and everyone else who worked shelter were still shaken from learning that one of their own was a serial killer. They all thought Evan seemed a little weird, but nothing like this had ever crossed their minds.

The door closed behind her, and she walked to her office. Amber set down the bagel sandwich and her pack. Next, she headed to the reception area, where she filled the coffee pot with water and poured it into the machine so that it would be ready in 20 minutes when her employees started arriving.

Returning to her office, she sat at her desk and was

unwrapping her breakfast when she became aware of someone standing in her doorway.

"Hi, Amber."

Amber's head jerked up, recognizing the voice, and her bladder released. As she glanced at the Taser in Evan's hand, the terror overwhelmed her, and she couldn't speak or move but felt it as a single tear ran down her face.

"I'm sorry to have to do this. You were always nice to me, but I needed one more target, and I always planned on you being my last one," the killer said.

The terrified woman's mouth opened to plead for her life, but no sound would come out.

Evan took a couple of steps forward, and Amber considered running, but he stood between her and the door. Then she noticed his other hand held a large spray can with an odd tube coming off it.

"This'll be easier if you stand up."

She didn't move.

"Amber, I said stand!"

This time she complied, not knowing what else to do. She understood that she now presented a better target.

The needle-like barbs struck as planned, and she heard the fast clicking sound the weapon made as she dropped to the ground, her body raked with hundreds of electrical jolts.

She couldn't move, but she knew Evan was kneeling at her side and could see his spray can moving closer.

Chapter 48

THE RED HONDA LEFT THE PARKING LOT WITH EVAN AT THE wheel and the unwrapped bagel sandwich in his hand.

This was the first time he'd felt any regret over killing. All the others had been strangers, not someone who'd always been friendly with him.

As soon as he'd finished with the spray can, he'd taken Amber's hand and sat holding it for the full minute and a half it had taken for her heart to stop. He hoped the gesture had been comforting to her in the end. Then he got up and, leaving the FoamX can behind, closed her office door and unlocked the main doors.

This should seem normal to those arriving for work. It wasn't uncommon for Amber to close herself in her office, limiting her distractions as she navigated the bureaucracy that came with her position. With any luck, it would be midmorning before anyone discovered her body.

Evan smiled as he drove. He now had transportation, money, breakfast, and he'd shown the police that their depriving him of his home couldn't stop him. Now he needed to avoid them for a while as he figured out his next steps.

Driving into the city, he parked in a municipal lot off of

East Broadway Boulevard. He walked the quarter-mile to the Greyhound bus station carrying the duffel bag he'd bought the evening before.

Entering the station, he went to a kiosk and started looking at bus routes. He wanted a distant destination with many stops that departed soon and settled on a bus going to Miami, Florida. The price was a little over $500, and it would take 60 hours to get there. The bus would depart in 20 minutes.

Taking a seat, he waited 10 minutes and then purchased the ticket with one of the prepaid debit cards, getting the small paper ticket from the machine.

Heading outside, he located the bus and took a seat in the loading area, watching the passengers board.

When the driver made a last call for anyone wanting to store bags in the cargo compartment, Evan took the duffle bag and, after showing his ticket to the driver, turned it over to be loaded.

Chapter 49

EARLY IN THE AFTERNOON, MAC STOOD IN THE OFFICE OF THE Tuscon Animal Shelter, looking at the dead woman on the ground. The familiar rigid yellow foam was protruding from the victim's mouth and nose.

She fought to control the rage and despair that needed release. She wanted to be by herself and smash something, but as the task force leader, she had to set an example for the others. George Jenkins and Dan Felty stood with her and were equally enraged.

A piece of computer paper was on the desk, with the empty FoamX can acting as a paperweight. The taunting nature of the note made them especially angry.

"Raiding my home won't stop me. Amber is only dead because of you. Evan"

Mac knew better than to feel responsible for the woman's death, but she still wondered if she should have done something differently.

The crime scene techs had finished their work, and the team from the medical examiner's office prepared to take Amber's body.

The detectives moved to the side and watched as two

women rolled in the stretcher and lowered it next to Evan's latest victim. They unfolded a heavy-duty black-vinyl body bag, placed it next to the corpse, and unzipped it. Respectfully, the team rolled Amber on to her left side and pushed the bag under her. After laying her flat again, they adjusted the bag and body until she rested in the center, and then zipped the bag closed.

The detectives watched as the bag was lifted to the stretcher and removed from the room.

After the crew had departed, Mac said, "Dan, remember when we spoke to the FBI profiler? He said we needed to do something to throw him off his game. Force him to reveal himself."

"Sure, I remember. That almost got me killed."

"True, but we did make him react to us. Let's try again. I have an idea. Are you up for a road trip?"

Chapter 50

JENNY MOORE HAD BEEN BACK IN TUSCON FOR ONLY A DAY and was now in a car headed to meet the rest of the team at the animal shelter. Her partner, Tom Koster, sat in the seat next to her.

Her phone rang, and she saw it was from Mac. She pressed a button, and the call was on the car's audio system for them both to hear.

"Hey, Mac. You're on with Tom and me. We're only about 10 min from the shelter."

"Change of plans. We're finishing up there now, and we just got the warrant for Evan's phone and are tracking it now. He's on Highway 10 headed north out of town.

"I want you guys to chase him down. I'm working on getting the tracking info sent directly to you, and we're getting a helicopter out of Phoenix to coordinate with you."

"Okay, do you know what he's driving? What kind of car are we looking for?" Jenny asked.

"A small red Honda belonging to the latest victim is missing. That's the best we have. For now, focus on catching up to the area the phone is in, and we'll figure the rest out as you drive."

After 20 minutes, Tom and Jenny received a message with a link. Tom took a tablet computer from his bag, powered it on, connected it to the department's network, and then opened the link.

A map appeared on the screen showing the state of Arizona and two moving dots.

Using his fingers, he zoomed in and could see both dots on highway 10. One was red and indicated the phone they were tracking, and the other was blue. That was their vehicle.

The speed each dot was moving appeared on the screen.

"You need to speed up. He's moving at about 80. We're closing in, but not by much," Tom instructed his partner.

Half an hour later, they'd closed the distance some but were still a good 15 minutes behind the moving dot.

Tom's phone rang, and he put it on the car's speakers.

"Hello?"

"This is Darren with the Phoenix Police Aviation Department. We're tracking the phone and have an aircraft over its location."

"Great, does your aircrew see a small red SUV?"

"No. They've been loitering over the area for 10 minutes, and the only vehicle that has been in the target area the whole time is a passenger bus."

Tom and Jenny looked at one another, and after consideration, Jenny nodded.

Tom said, "We are a good 15 minutes behind. Can you get the bus stopped?"

Fourteen minutes later, Jenny saw a swarm of blue lights ahead and started slowing and pulled to the side of the road behind a half-dozen SUVs from the Arizona Department of Public Safety.

Exiting, they approached a bus stopped on the side of the road. The cargo compartment had been emptied, and baggage sat in a row up along the side of the bus. A canine officer was walking along the row of bags, investigating each piece.

A uniformed trooper with lieutenant's bars on his collar approached.

"Are you Moore and Koster?"

"Yes, we are. What've you found?" Jenny asked.

"All the passengers are on the bus. You can check for yourselves, but none matches the photo of your suspect, and we have looked at all their IDs. He isn't there."

"What about the phone?" Tom inquired.

"We found it in a bag in the cargo compartment. All that was in the bag was the phone and a sweatshirt with the tags still on it. It looks like the sweatshirt was only in the bag to keep it from looking empty. I think this was all a decoy to distract your investigation."

Chapter 51

BRIAN CONNOR LOOKED AT THE CARDS IN HIS HAND AND inwardly smiled at what he'd been dealt. He had two black Jacks, two red aces, and a red nine. He and his partner needed only one more point, and the game of euchre would be won. Since the person on his right had dealt and turned up a black 10, victory was guaranteed.

As an inmate at the Lewisburg Federal Prison Camp in Pennsylvania, Brian had won and lost thousands of card games in the 15 years he'd been incarcerated.

Two levels of single-occupancy cells surrounded the common area where the inmates were playing. The doors to the cells were seldom closed. Because of this, card games were going on almost 24 hours a day.

This specific cell block was known as a no-problem area. The inmates here were non-violent; all kept their heads down and followed the rules. None of them wanted to do anything to risk being moved to a stricter environment. In all the years Brian had been incarcerated, he'd never received a reprimand.

He'd made sure that these kinds of accommodations were agreed upon before he provided testimony against the cartel he'd laundered money for. In exchange, he'd not held anything back and given federal prosecutors everything he knew.

To protect him in prison, he served his sentence under the alias Kevin Baker. No one, not even the warden, knew his real identity.

As Brian told the dealer to pick up the turned-over card, one of the corrections officers walked up and spoke to him, "Hey, Kev. Finish up the hand. I need you to come with me."

"Sure. What's up?" Brian asked, the confusion evident in his voice. There was a regular routine in prison, and this was unusual.

"You have visitors."

His partner in the card game spoke up, "Today isn't a visiting day."

"These people aren't that kind of visitors," the corrections officer said.

Confused and intrigued, the inmate set the cards down, not even taking the 10 seconds needed to secure the final point to win the game. He stood and followed the officer.

"We can finish when I get back," he told the other players.

The door to the cell block clicked open as they approached, controlled by someone in the operations center on the other side of the facility. It closed behind them with a loud clang.

"Hey, Dave, any idea what this is about?" Brian asked, as they walked up the corridor.

"No. The supervisor just told me to fetch you. I saw three guys, two in suits. One of them might have been the attorney you met with a few months back," the officer said.

"Well, I'm up for parole again in a couple of months. It's probably related to my upcoming hearing."

They continued further up the corridor and waited as the door to the interview room opened.

Brian stepped inside and saw three men. One of the men

in a suit was Daren Bilks, his attorney. The others he didn't recognize.

"Hey, Daren. I wasn't expecting to see you until closer to my parole hearing. Is there news?"

"This isn't related. However, it may help your chances for release," the lawyer said. "This is agent Codden with the US Marshals Service and Detective Felty from the Tucson Police Department."

"Tucson? I've never even been to Arizona."

Dan nodded. "I know."

The lawyer continued, "These guys have given me the basics but can't go into details with me here. Even though I'm your lawyer, I shouldn't know your former identity. If you help them, both the US marshals and Tucson PD agree to send positive recommendations to the parole board. You came close to getting out last time. If you have the support from these agencies, I think there's a great chance you'll be out in a couple of months."

"I understand. Thanks, Daren," the inmate said.

Brian sat across from the other men as the lawyer left the room. While the corrections officers weren't in the room and couldn't hear the conversation, they monitored the meeting by video in case of unexpected trouble.

Marshal Codden started by asking, "Do you want us to call you Brian or Kevin?"

"Brian, please. The only people who call me Kevin are in this prison, and I'll leave that name behind when I eventually walk out the door."

"That's fine. I'm your case officer. You worked with Marshal Delange when you came here, and she's since moved on. The service hasn't had reason to contact you, so there's no reason you would've known."

Brian nodded. "It's been over 14 years, so that makes sense."

The marshal continued, "When you started cooperating

with the marshal's service, we cut off all contact with your family at your request. They could never contact you because they were relocated and had new identities. We agreed it would be safer for them if you also didn't know about them."

"That's right. I figured it was better this way until I got out. Then I'd try to find them," Brian confirmed.

Dan asked, "So you haven't heard anything about them or where they went when relocated?"

"That's right. Why? Are they okay?" The concern was evident in the inmate's voice.

The marshal shook his head. "We agreed we wouldn't communicate their status to you, but something has come up, and we need your help. So, we need to tell you about them, and it isn't good."

Brian's voice trembled as he spoke. "Tell me. I need to know."

Chapter 52

BRIAN CONNOR'S HEAD RESTED ON THE TABLE IN THE interview room as he wept uncontrollably. For almost 15 years, he'd dreamed of reuniting with his family. Possibly even picking up where they'd left off. He'd now learned that the college sweetheart he'd gone on to marry, and their precious daughter, had died 12 years earlier.

When he'd composed himself, he asked, "You said Blake was injured in the crash. How bad? Did he survive?"

"Broken bones, which all healed well. He went on to live in a series of foster homes until he graduated and went to college. These weren't bad foster home situations, but he didn't fit into any well enough to stay permanently," Marshal Codden said.

"He was such a wonderful boy. He and I did everything together. Back then, I thought it would be like that forever."

After a pause, he looked at Dan and asked, "Where is he now? Tucson?"

Dan nodded. "Last we knew. This is the part where we need your help."

"Has he done something wrong?" the concerned father asked.

"A serial killer has been terrorizing Tucson for a couple of months. Fourteen attacks with 11 people killed. We have verified the killer is Evan Brown. That's the name the marshal service gave Blake when they relocated him."

"That sounds like a common name. How do you know your Evan is Blake?" The desperate father asked as the color drained from his face.

Marshal Codden said, "We record the DNA of anyone entering WITSEC. The marshal's service received an alert when the Tucson PD ran a search on their subject's DNA from blood left at one of the murders. It's certain."

Brian lurched to the left and vomited on the floor.

This morning when he awoke in his cell, he'd had hope. Hope he could one day reconnect with his lost family. With one conversation, his hope disappeared. Four million dollars awaited him in a bank account in the Cayman Islands, but what value did that money have if the people who mattered to him were lost?

He wept again as he thought of his incredible son, Blake, and what had happened to him.

"How did this happen? Can you explain any of it?" Brian pleaded.

The marshal took several seconds to formulate his answer. "No one can say for sure, but two key things seemed to trigger all of this. First, your wife didn't adjust well to her new life. It's never easy, but she had a terrible time, which led to her making poor choices. The second was the death of your daughter, which devastated Evan. He lay right there and couldn't do anything. The reports from those who treated him indicate he blamed himself for being unable to save her."

A full minute of silence passed before Brian straightened himself up in the chair and said, "So, what's it you want from me?"

Dan answered, "Evan is on the run, and we don't know where he'll go."

"I haven't seen him since he was nine years old. I don't know where he'd go. Maybe our old home outside Chicago."

"We're watching the Chicago address," the marshal said.

"But that isn't what we're looking for," Dan said. "We know he's following the investigation online, and we're hoping you would record a message to him. Encourage him to make contact. One way or another, we need to stop him, but with your help, maybe we can keep him alive."

Chapter 53

IT WAS EARLY MORNING, AND EVAN HAD SPENT THE LAST TWO nights in a cheap roadside motel. He'd worked out a plan but wanted to be sure he wouldn't need to return to the area before moving on.

He'd lived in Tucson for the past two years and was reluctant to leave the area. This was the first time he felt like he had a home in a long time. However, leaving had become a necessity.

The news stations were showing his photo along with his current and birth name to the public. He could only do so much to disguise himself. It wouldn't be long before someone recognized him.

Knowing it could be tracked by GPS, he'd left the red Honda running outside a rundown convenience store before checking into the motel. He felt confident someone would quickly steal it.

Fast food and Chinese takeout containers littered the room as Evan sat on the bed in his underwear, taking advantage of the slow but free wifi.

He used his tablet to access the website of a Tucson TV station, went to the news tab, and looked for information on the status of the investigation. He found a new article titled, *"Serial Killing Suspect's Father Reaches Out From Prison."*

Evan stared at the title and was confused by what he saw. After several seconds, a video opened, and he had to wait while the sluggish internet connection downloaded the contents.

He saw a single man in an empty room. He wore an orange jumpsuit with lettering on the front left, which wasn't clear enough to read. However, the man's face was familiar, and Evan paused the recording and stared at the father he hadn't seen since he'd been a child. As the emotions washed over him, he wasn't sure if he wanted to keep watching.

While he gazed at the face, memories came flooding back. Memories of activities the two of them had done together. Times when they were playing in the pool and occasions all four of them had spent as a family. The clearest memory was the day his father left and his saying he wouldn't be coming back.

Evan understood his dad hadn't chosen to leave and that he'd been in prison. However, he still felt bitterness toward the man who'd meant so much to him and all that was lost because of his imprisonment.

Clicking the play button again, Evan watched and listened to the personal message.

"Hi, Blake. I've missed you so much. It's been agonizing all these years, not knowing where you were and not having a way to reach out to you. I've been dreaming of the day when I'll be released and can find you. That day is coming soon. I want to hear about your life and what you've been dealing with.

"But I understand there are some problems you're involved in and, for us to connect again, we need to deal with them. There's a phone number I need you to call. They've assured me they'll allow us to talk if you call and speak to the authorities.

"I love you very much and want to see you again. I need to explain what happened and why I had to go away. You deserve to hear it directly from me. Please call the number on the screen."

At the end of the video, a phone number appeared on the display. Evan took a screenshot and then watched the video again seven times.

The most impactful part of the message was being called Blake. It sounded out of place and familiar at the same time, and it brought back more memories.

Evan wasn't sure what to do, but he knew he needed to speak to his father, no matter what it took.

Chapter 54

THE TASK FORCE AGAIN GATHERED IN THE CONFERENCE ROOM. It had been three days since there'd been any changes in the case, and they all feared Evan would strike again soon.

It had taken most of a day to find the phone he'd planted on the Greyhound bus bound for Miami, and frustrations increased when, as expected, it had been a decoy. The small duffle bag that held the phone was being examined in the crime lab, but no one expected it to reveal much.

Evan had wiped the phone clean of data before hiding it in the bag. Still, the detectives hoped something would be recoverable.

Mac displayed the report from Amber Goddard's autopsy on the screen for the team to see, but there hadn't been anything unexpected in it.

The only positive news was that the photo of Evan was now being circulated, and the video from his father was available for download from the news sites.

As the detectives discussed their situation and brainstormed ideas, an officer stuck his head in, "Hey, Mac! There's someone on the hotline you should talk to."

"Thanks. Transfer it in here," she instructed, wondering if this might be Evan calling in.

When the phone on the table rang, everyone stopped talking, and Mac pressed the speaker button.

"This is Detective Bell. Who am I speaking to?"

"I'm Denny Fox. I work at the Peaceful Rest Motel up by Oro Valley. The guy on the news is staying here."

"Denny, why do you think it's him?" Mac asked, trying to keep her voice neutral.

"I'm the one who checked him in a couple of days ago. I saw him clearly, and then today, I saw the photo online. It's him. Also, I told him I needed his ID to rent him a room. He said he lost his license but showed me a birth certificate. Now, that isn't really allowed, but I wasn't sure what else to do, so I made a copy of it and checked him in."

"What's the name on the birth certificate?"

"Blake Connor. That's one of the names I saw online with the photo of this guy."

"What room is he in?"

"58."

"Don't go near the room but have a key ready for the officers who arrive. We're on our way," Mac said, now unable to keep the excitement out of her voice.

With no instructions needed, the task force members sprinted toward the parking lot.

As they ran, Mac dialed her phone.

"Hey, Mac. Any news?" Lieutenant Miller asked when he answered her call.

"I need you to call Oro Valley. Tell them we're on our way. We strongly believe Evan is staying in room 58 in the Peaceful Rest Motel. I need them to secure the perimeter immediately. If they decide to go in, there's a key waiting in the motel office."

"I'll call them now. Good luck."

Mac disconnected, hoping their neighboring department

would wait to enter until they arrived, but she knew that probably wouldn't happen. Everyone understood that stopping Evan was the priority, not who made the arrest.

Because of morning commuter traffic, even with emergency lights on, it took the task force close to 20 minutes to reach the motel.

As they pulled in, they saw four marked vehicles from the Oro Valley Police Department in the side lot. Their emergency lights were on, and they were parked at various angles in front of room 58.

As Mac exited her vehicle, she saw an officer coming out of room 58 with a frustrated expression. Mac's enthusiasm died.

A female officer with sergeant's stripes on her uniform sleeves shook her head as she walked up.

"I'm Mackenzie Bell, the task force commander," Mac greeted her.

The women shook hands.

"Beth McKellen. Your guy left before we got here. The place is a mess, but there are no personal effects. I don't think he's coming back. You need to check the bathroom. It looks like he's trying to change his appearance."

The disappointment was etched on Mac's face. "Thanks for securing the room. I'd hoped we'd show up and see him in the back of your cruiser, in cuffs."

"Yeah, we wanted that, too. I can't say why, but I got the feeling he hasn't been gone long. I have all our people on the lookout."

The rest of the team joined her, and she pointed at Tom Koster and Jenny Moore. "You two go in. We don't need everyone in there until the crime-scene unit finishes."

As the two detectives headed in, Sergeant McKellen said, "Once we were sure he'd gone, I pulled our people out."

Mac nodded. "Thanks for getting here so fast."

Minutes later, as the women were still speaking, Tom

Koster approached with a clear evidence bag. "Mac, check this out."

"What is it?"

"It's a package of temporary tattoos. It's open, and there's one missing. Not sure what it is. They aren't any descriptions on the packaging. We found it in the bathroom with a pair of barber clippers and a bunch of hair," Detective Koster explained.

Mac took the bag and asked, "Has this been photographed yet?"

"Of course. I wouldn't have brought it out if it hadn't been," Koster replied indignantly.

Turning to Detective Jenkins, Mac said, "George. Find out where this is sold and get an identical package. We need to know what the missing tattoo is. It looks like Evan shaved his head and put the tattoo on as a disguise."

As they were talking, Mac's phone rang.

"This is Bell."

"Mac, this is Tanya in communications. There's another hotline call for you. He says he's Evan."

Chapter 55

EVAN HAD GOTTEN DRESSED, GATHERED UP HIS BELONGINGS, and using the tablet, requested a car using a popular rideshare app.

When the car arrived at the motel, the driver already knew the destination and took him to a local shopping mall.

As he rode, he watched as three police SUVs screamed past, going in the opposite direction.

Arriving at the mall, Evan went inside, located the bank of elevators that went to the upper level, and took a seat watching. It only took a few minutes to find what he needed. A group of four teenagers headed to the elevators, and among them was a girl with a cell phone sticking half out of her back pocket. They were all talking and laughing. Evan got up and followed. When they entered the elevator, he did too, bumping into the girl.

"Excuse me. I'm sorry," Evan said with a grin.

She glanced at him with a pretty smile which quickly disappeared as she turned away, avoiding looking at him. Evan smiled inwardly; his change of appearance had the desired effect.

When the teens left the elevator, Evan rode it back down with the girl's phone in his hand.

Leaving the mall, he walked a short distance to where he could board a city bus and got on the first one to arrive, not caring where he was headed.

He made his way to the back of the bus, took an empty seat, and accessed the phone, which fortunately didn't have a passcode set.

He dialed the number he'd seen at the end of his father's recording and heard a woman's voice answer, "Tucson police hotline."

"This is Evan Brown. I need to talk to my father."

"Okay, I'm transferring you," the woman said, anxiety appearing in her voice.

It took 20 seconds before another woman answered, "Evan?"

"I need to speak to my father."

"I'm Detective Bell, and you and I need to talk first."

"Are you the short detective who's been looking for me and searched my house? The one whose partner I shot?"

"Yes, Evan, that's me. I need you to turn yourself in before things get worse."

"Not before I talk to my dad."

"Evan, that's not how it works. You come in and talk to me and I promise I'll get you on the phone with your dad within an hour."

So far, the conversation had progressed as Evan expected it would. By now, they most certainly were trying to trace the call.

"I'm hanging up now. I'll call back in five days, at 4 pm. You have my dad available then, and after he and I talk, I'll tell you where to find me. That's how it'll work, or there'll be more bodies."

Evan disconnected the call, shoved the phone between the

seat and the bus wall where it would be hard to find, and got off at the next stop.

He waited while two other buses came and went, wanting to distance himself from the phone he'd abandoned. He then felt comfortable boarding the next bus, which he took to a transfer point, where he caught yet another bus heading back downtown. It was time to leave the area. His plan required it.

Chapter 56

EVAN AWOKE, HAVING SLEPT SOUNDLY AS THE GREYHOUND BUS made its way along the dark highway. He was on day two of a three-day journey and had already changed buses three times. There'd be two more transfers before he reached his destination.

So far, his disguise had proven to have an added benefit. People tended to avoid sitting next to a skinhead with a gruesome skull tattooed on his face. So, unless there were no other seats open during a specific leg of the trip, the one next to him remained empty.

As he rode, he spent lots of time thinking about his situation. He was still stunned the police had identified him, and he spent hours pondering what he'd done wrong to allow them to figure it out.

He assumed the spray can he dropped, when the woman shot him, allowed them to track him. Leaving it behind was a stupid mistake. He knew the cans had numbers on the bottom and suspected that had been the clue they needed to identify him.

Still, he was sure the cops were banging their heads,

wondering where he was now and what he'd be doing for the five days between calls.

The bus pulled off the highway and moved through a town. Evan was tempted to look at his tablet to see where they were, but he didn't bother.

The driver announced the bus would be stopping for 15 minutes if anyone wanted to get off and stretch their legs.

At most of the stops, he hadn't, but this time he did, leaving his bag on his seat. It was a small bus station with nothing more than a restroom and some vending machines.

Exiting the restroom, he got a can of soda and two packs of salted peanuts from the machines and got back on the bus, surprised to see someone sitting in the seat next to him.

The man was disheveled and in his sixties. Evan excused himself and moved past the man to the window seat where his bag was.

As he settled in, Evan looked at the man, who reeked of cigarette smoke. Then he closed his eyes and fantasized about his seatmate, wishing he had a Taser and a can of FoamX.

Chapter 57

First thing in the morning, Mac walked from her house into the garage. Her phone chimed with a text. She paused before looking at it, fearing it would say Evan had killed again. When she did look at the screen, her stomach dropped.

She had to report to Lieutenant Miller as soon as she arrived at the office. She had a strong suspicion about the meeting topic, and she wasn't happy.

Mac felt exhausted. The daily increases in her feelings of failure kept her awake at night.

She backed her car out of the garage and headed directly to work, wanting to get this meeting over with.

Walking into the midtown detective bureau, she knocked on her supervisor's door and stepped inside. "Morning, Lieutenant," she said.

"Take a seat, Mac."

She sat, and he continued, "I got a call from Chief Sawyer last night. He made the decision. The department has officially asked the FBI to assist us in the investigation."

Mac inwardly cringed; her suspicions were correct.

Reading her body language, Miller added, "They're coming to assist, not take over."

"That's what they say now," the dejected detective replied.

"No. The chief made it clear that we were continuing to lead the investigation, but while we've made great progress, a fresh set of eyes is desired."

"It makes me feel you and the chief don't have confidence in me and my team."

"I've been working right alongside you on this, and I think the moves you've made are correct, and I told that to the chief. But this needs to be brought to a close, and if the feds can bring fresh ideas or tools we can use, we can't let ego allow Evan to kill again."

Mac knew her boss was right, but that didn't make the feeling of failure fade.

"I'm going to go and tell the team," Mac said. "Do you know when the feds will be arriving?"

"Sometime tomorrow. They'll be reporting to you. Are you still expecting Evan's call in two days?"

"Yeah, I think he'll call. He'd better – it's the only plan we have."

Chapter 58

EVAN DISEMBARKED IN WOLF CREEK, MONTANA, THREE DAYS after boarding the bus in Arizona. The ticket he'd purchased would have taken him three more stops. He'd intentionally purchased a ticket going farther than necessary in case the police were tracking him.

Walking from the bus stop, he saw a diner and headed inside, thankful for the chance for a decent meal after three days on the road.

He walked to the back and took a booth facing the door.

Glancing over the menu, he decided on a simple burger and fries.

A young waitress brought him his food, then stayed away, obviously uncomfortable with his appearance. The disguise which kept him from being recognized in Arizona made him stand out here in Montana.

After finishing a mediocre meal, he left the restaurant and headed to a regional department store. He went to the clothing section, where he bought two complete outfits. He hadn't changed his clothes in a week and was offending himself after the long bus ride.

Moving on, he went to the sporting goods department and

spent a full 10 minutes picking out a big backpack. He wanted a large one that sat comfortably, and it needed to have a strap to go around his waist.

The one he selected was blue and a little smaller than he wanted, but it seemed the most comfortable.

Next, he picked out a small cook stove, insect repellent, a tent and a sleeping bag.

Moving to the back wall, he looked at the fishing poles and selected a collapsible one in a case, along with a small kit of various lures.

Evan wasn't sure if they were the right lures for what he needed and didn't really care. He'd gone fishing only twice before and hadn't enjoyed it.

Heading to the grocery section, he found enough prepared food to last him several days and a case of water bottles.

Before checking out, he located the last two items he needed, a disposable cell phone and two tubes of superglue.

He paid for his gear using one of the two prepaid credit cards he'd dug up in his backyard.

Evan planned to hike most of the day with his full backpack, but a pickup truck driven by an older woman stopped right after he started walking.

"Hey, do you need a ride?" the woman asked.

From the angle she was at, she couldn't see the temporary facial tattoo.

Evan considered the offer for a moment before responding. "That'd be great," he said. "I'm going about 15 miles east to the hiking trails along the river, if you are heading that way."

"I'll be going right past there. Toss your stuff in the back and get in."

Evan did as asked and relaxed for the 15-minute drive to the trailhead, glad the woman didn't talk much.

The truck dropped him at a trailhead and, from there, he

had a short 20-minute walk and arrived at his destination. It was a small rustic camping area along a river.

Evan remembered this place well. He'd camped here twice with his stepfather. The last time was two weeks before the accident that had killed his family.

Most of his memories of Ray Williams, other than when he fought with his mother, were positive. The man had some problems, but he'd tried to build a relationship with young Evan.

Those pleasant memories are what brought the killer from Tuscon back to this camping area. He figured he'd camp and fish in memory of Ray while waiting the remaining day until the time came to call and speak to his father.

Locating an abandoned campsite with a circle of rocks used for a campfire, Evan pitched his tent and then gathered wood for the fire.

He lit the fire and then sat back, enjoying the smell of the burning wood and the memories it brought back. The enjoyment didn't last long before other emotions were triggered, and Evan wept uncontrollably as he thought of not only his sister but also his mother and stepfather.

Chapter 59

Noon approached, and Evan sat on the bank of the river eating ravioli from a can he'd heated on his camp stove. It was nearing time to pack and leave. The day-and-a-half had been relaxing, but now he was bored.

He returned to the tent and dumped everything he had brought out of the backpack. He wouldn't be needing anything in there. He glanced at the still-sealed fishing pole. He'd never bothered even to try using it.

He stuck the disposable phone in his pocket. After some final preparations, he put on the backpack and walked off carrying a single bottle of water in his hand.

Not familiar with the trails in the area, he walked along the roadway and arrived at his new destination after a little over three hours. A three-foot strip of unkempt grass separated the roadway and the steep slope that led to the water below.

Evan walked to a specific spot on the bank and considered lying down, but he didn't want to remove the backpack.

This was the same place he'd lain years before, with broken bones, as he watched his sister, mother, and stepfather drown.

Several times in the years that followed, he'd run away from the foster homes to spend the night sleeping in this spot.

After a few minutes, he headed to where the land dropped off into the deep part of the lake and looked down, reminiscing, while tears ran down his face.

One of his foster families had bothered to learn why this spot was important to him, and after that, they'd driven him here a few times. He thought about that family now and wished he could have stopped to see them again. Of the four families he had stayed with while in the foster system, they were his favorite.

Most of the time, when Evan thought about his sister, sorrow overcame him, but not when he was here. This place evoked another emotion, anger.

The longer he remained here, the angrier he got. Angry because his mother and stepfather caused the accident with their drunkenness. He was also angry because he and his sister had to endure their frequent fighting. Still, thinking of his real father caused most of the anger. His actions had caused his mother to have to move here in the first place.

Walking to a stump, Evan took a seat; the backpack was becoming uncomfortable.

After sitting for about 20 minutes, he checked his watch and saw it was about time to make his call.

Standing up, Evan dug the phone from his pocket and started dialing. Before he finished making the call, he stopped when he saw two men approaching.

The new arrivals were still 25 yards away, but they both seemed familiar and were heading directly toward him.

They both wore long pants, and the younger had a light-blue polo shirt. The older wore a faded T-shirt with wording that wasn't immediately decipherable and had a device strapped around his left ankle. Seconds later, Evan's brain connected the dots and his eyes went wide as questions came rushing in.

As they got closer, Evan could see the T-shirt read, "Inmate Pennsylvania Department of Corrections."

Not sure what to say to the older man, Evan looked specifically at the younger man, "Well, Detective. I see you survived."

"Yes, Evan, I did," Dan Felty responded.

"How'd you know I'd be here?"

"Your foster-care records documented your desire to return here frequently."

Unable to delay any longer, he looked at the other man — the man he loved and hated at the same time.

Then he realized what his father must be thinking and felt embarrassed to stand there with a shaved head and a skull tattooed on his face.

"Hello, Dad."

Chapter 60

BRIAN CONNOR HAD EAGERLY ACCEPTED THE OPPORTUNITY TO travel to Montana for the possibility of seeing his son again. The long trip would be worth it if he could talk Blake into surrendering peacefully. He was thankful Dan Felty had arranged it.

With his parole all but guaranteed, there was little concern he wouldn't behave and that he'd damage his chances for release.

The trip had taken 27 hours and, since Brian didn't have a driver's license, the detective did all the driving. However, the men talked most of the way and had almost become friends.

Brian Connor smiled at the son he hadn't seen in 14 years. "Hi, Blake. I've missed you so much," he said softly.

Evan shook his head vigorously. "Don't you call me that! You took that name away from me."

The response surprised Brian. He hadn't expected his son to run up and hug him after all this time, but he wasn't prepared for the hostility. He'd need to stay focused and tread carefully. Talking his son into a peaceful surrender was all that mattered. He understood Detective Felty wouldn't let his

Blake escape and would shoot to kill if needed. Also, there were six cars from the Montana State Police a quarter mile up the road if needed, all monitoring the situation.

"Okay, I won't call you Blake. But you're my son, and I love you. We used to have so much fun together."

"I remember some of it. Mom used to tell me about those times so I wouldn't forget," Evan acknowledged.

"That doesn't surprise me. She was a wonderful woman. I miss her terribly."

"What about Patti? Do you miss her too? She was so scared when you left. She cried for days. She'd only stop crying when I held her."

Brian was momentarily confused by the name Patti. He'd only ever thought of his daughter by the name Cindy. The name she had until they relocated her.

"Of course, I miss her, too. You guys meant everything to me."

Unimpressed by the statement, Evan said, "Do you know what this place is? Do you know what happened here?"

"I know this is where they died. It's where you were injured."

"Come here, Dad," Evan said forcefully, walking closer to the center of the clearing.

Brian followed.

"Right here is where I lay while they drowned. My leg was broken in three places, so I couldn't help them. I lay here all night looking at the spot they went in, begging for them to come to the surface. But that never happened," Evan wept as he explained.

"We can spend as much time as you want discussing this, but I need you to come with me and Detective Felty," Brian Connor told his insane son.

"I know, but first, I need you to see something."

He reached out his hand. "Come with me, Dad."

Brian looked at the detective, who nodded his consent.

He took the offered hand, overjoyed to touch his son again, and thankful Detective Felty allowed this moment.

Evan led him to the edge overlooking the water, with the detective following a short distance back.

"Is this where the car went in?" Brian asked with tears in his own eyes.

"It was a van. But yeah, this is where it happened." Evan's tears returned, and he pulled closer to his father, who took him in his arms.

Brian was overjoyed to hold his son again.

"I love you, Dad," the younger man said.

Then, without warning, Evan grabbed his father in a tight bear hug and launched the two of them off the edge and they fell into the water below.

As they sank, Evan wrapped his legs around his father, trapping him in a python-like grip.

This had always been Evan's exit plan, but he never imagined his father would be here, too.

The 90 pounds of rocks from around the campfire were now in the backpack and rapidly pulled the two men the 18 feet to the bottom.

Brian heard someone else entering the water and assumed it was Detective Felty, but they had sunk quickly and were now quite deep. He doubted the detective could reach them in time.

Realizing he couldn't break his son's grip, Brian grabbed at the plastic clasps holding the backpack's straps tight. But Evan had been concerned that he might panic and change his mind once in the water, so he'd squirted copious amounts of super glue in the clasps. Not understanding this, Brian fought unsuccessfully against them.

As he became aware of his strength fading, his son rolled the dying father over, so Evan's weight and the pack held him to the bottom. Even if Evan passed out first, Brian would still be trapped.

Accepting his fate, he gazed into his son's face one last time and saw nothing but joy and contentment looking back at him.

Chapter 61

DAN SMILED AS HIS PLAN TO USE EVAN'S FATHER TO GET HIM to surrender seemed to be working. The men were talking and expressing emotions. It seemed as if Evan might surrender if that meant being able to maintain contact with his father.

Dan had developed a fondness for Brian and hoped he'd be able to have a relationship with his son, even if that were only in the way of prison visitations.

Evan and Brian walked closer to the water, and Dan felt a chill. Something was bothering him. Something he couldn't place.

As he walked with them, staying about 15 yards back, he realized what it was. The backpack. It was clear to see by how it sat that it was very heavy, but Evan hadn't removed it when he got here to make the call. What would be so valuable that he'd keep it on despite the discomfort?

The men embraced at the edge, where it dropped into the deep water, and now the mental alarm was screaming that something was wrong.

Before he could act, the father and son went over the edge and into the water.

Stunned for a second, Dan sprinted to the water's edge

while grabbing for his hip and the radio the Montana State Police had provided him.

"Need help, two men down in the water!"

He dropped the radio and kicked off his shoes. Removing his gun, he dropped it with the radio and dived headfirst into the water.

Following the trail of bubbles, he propelled himself down, deep into the cold water, searching for the men.

Just when he thought he needed to return to the surface, Dan saw the father and son lying on the bottom.

They were both flat on the lake bed, and Evan was on top of Brian. The two men lay next to the wrecked bumper that had come off a minivan over a decade earlier.

Grabbing Evan by the arm, Dan tried to lift him off his father, but whatever was in the backpack was too heavy.

Adjusting his position, as his lungs screamed for oxygen, Dan managed to roll Evan off the unmoving form of Brian Connor.

Lifting Brian from under his shoulders, Dan tried to push off from the ground to propel them towards the surface, but his strength failed, and Evan's father slipped from his grasp.

As Dan tried to grab him again, his vision faded as his oxygen-deprived brain shut down.

Chapter 62

As Dan regained consciousness for the second time in as many weeks, his first realization was that he was very cold.

He heard sirens approaching and became aware that he was flat on the ground with an oxygen mask on his face.

Still confused, he heard voices to his left and turned his head and saw a soaking-wet Montana State Trooper who was counting out loud as he repeatedly compressed the chest of another soaked man who was lying on the ground.

Dan saw the man's profile and knew it was Brian Connor. The events came rushing back, and he tried to get up, only to have another wet trooper press a firm hand on his shoulder. He lay back down.

"You aren't going anywhere. You were unconscious when we pulled you out of the water," the trooper said.

"What about Evan?" Dan asked as he started coughing.

"He's still on the bottom. We couldn't get him up to the surface and needed to focus on you two. We have a dive team coming; they'll recover the body," the trooper explained.

Feeling the need to help, Dan tried to get up again, only to be pushed down harder.

"Lie back down, Detective. We have it under control.

You've already made a big enough mess of things," the trooper ordered.

Dan lay back down, feeling like a failure, and watched as the EMTs ran up and started getting Brian loaded on a stretcher.

Chapter 63
TWO WEEKS LATER

Brooke Mitchell looked up from her paperwork when her phone chimed with a call.

Brooke was a senior evidence technician working in the Tucson Police Department crime lab. She was 34 years old and had been working as an evidence technician since leaving the Air Force eight years before.

Answering the call, she said, "This is Brooke."

The voice on the other end said, "Hey Brooke, this is Kenny in dispatch. We need you to meet Detective Lopez out on Grove Street near Pinewood. I'm sending the info to your van."

"Sure. Am I taking the whole team?"

"No, this is just a missing-person investigation that's been open for several weeks. There's no sign of foul play, but the guy has been gone long enough that we're taking a closer look."

"Okay, I'll be on my way in a couple of minutes," Brooke said as she disconnected the call.

She finished up the form she was working on, logged out of the computer, and headed to the refrigerator in the corner of the room. She took out a 20oz soda bottle and headed outside to her van.

As she pulled out of the fenced-in lot, she tapped the display screen on the dashboard, and navigational information appeared, including turn-by-turn directions on how to get to the address.

Seventeen minutes later, she arrived and parked behind the unmarked police SUV at the curb. As she put the vehicle in park, a middle age Hispanic man stepped out of the SUV.

"Hey, Brooke," he said in greeting.

Smiling at her colleague, she replied, "How you been, Danny?"

"I've been good," Danny Lopez answered.

"So, what's the story here?" the evidence technician asked.

"Missing person. A Mr. Charlie Dexter lives here alone. He failed to pick up his daughter for visitation almost three weeks ago. Apparently, that isn't something he'd normally fail to do. His ex-wife tried to contact him with no luck, so she called his employer, who said he had been a no-show for the previous four days.

"She knew where he kept a key and came over and looked through the house. There's no sign of a problem, but his truck is in the driveway. The ex filed a missing-person report over a week ago.

"I need you to process the house and truck to make sure there isn't something we're missing."

"Sure, no problem. Anything else I should know?" Brooke asked.

"Yeah. You'll find the back door damaged. Apparently, there was a home invasion here. Someone broke in through the back when Mr. Dexter was at work. The responding officers cleared the house and found nothing. It looks like they might have been the last ones to see Charlie before he disappeared."

"Are you thinking that the break-in was related to the disappearance?" Brooke asked.

"I would think so, but there's nothing so far to link them. That's why I want you here. Find the link if there is one. I already spoke to the officers who were here the night of the break-in, and they said that when they left, the house was clear, and Charlie was fine.

"You start your exam of the house and truck, and I'll be talking to the neighbors," the detective instructed.

"Sounds good," Brooke said as she turned and went back to her van. She removed two large bags with shoulder straps and headed inside.

Walking carefully in case there was evidence of a crime, she headed to the kitchen and placed the bags on the dining room table after carefully examining its surface. She took a large digital camera and a handheld light from one bag. She put on gloves and started a slow, painstaking examination of the main living areas. She photographed every room from multiple angles. As she headed down the hall, she noticed marks on the carpet near the bedroom. It looked like the area had recently been vacuum cleaned. Looking at the rest of the hall, she saw no such marks. Brooke glanced in the master bedroom, near where the marks in the hall were. She saw that the first three feet into the bedroom had also been vacuumed, but not the rest of the room.

It appeared to Brooke as if only the small area of the floor between the bedroom and the hall had been cleaned. The vacuum left impressions on the carpet that hadn't yet been disturbed by too many people walking on it.

Getting on her hands and knees, she looked more closely at the cleaned area. At first, she saw nothing, then up against the baseboard, there was a small light-blue object. Following the baseboards where a vacuum would have trouble getting, she spotted several more, one pink and another blue. Brooke knew what these were. Taser AFIDs.

With an idea of what happened here, she took a pair of tweezers, picked up one of the light blue objects, and took it back to the dining room table. Using her phone camera, she zoomed in on the AFID. She could read the series of numbers and letters repeatedly printed on its surface.

She removed a tablet computer from one of her bags, logged into her system back in the lab, and searched for the serial number. She felt a chill run down her spine when the results came back.

Taking out her phone, she dialed into the dispatch center.

"Hey, Brooke," the dispatcher said, recognizing her number.

"Kenny. Now I need my full forensics team here. Also, contact Detective Lopez and get him back here and find out if Mackenzie Bell is available to stop out."

Chapter 64

MACKENZIE BELL SAT IN THE DRIVER'S SEAT AND LOOKED OVER at her new partner. Newly promoted Detective Amanda Visser was thrilled that her promotion to detective had come through. She was also glad she got to work with someone she already liked. This was her first week out of uniform, and she was smart enough to tread lightly.

Mac and Dan Felty had been partners and friends for several years, and Mac wasn't taking Dan's suspension well. Technically they were calling it paid administrative leave, but there was little difference.

Dan had been responsible for a federal prisoner who was critically injured, and the Department of Justice demanded action.

Mac turned on to Grove Street and stopped behind another detective's vehicle and a van from the crime lab.

They headed up the walk and through the front door, which was slightly ajar. Not hearing anything, Amanda called out, "Hello."

"In the garage," a distant male voice called back.

The pair headed into the house, found the door to the garage off the hall, and entered, seeing Detective Danny

Lopez and Brook Mitchell from the crime lab standing by an open chest freezer.

"Just when we thought it was over, your friend Evan reappears," Danny said.

Confused, Mac walked over and looked into the freezer, her eyes going wide at what she saw. A face-up, frozen man was staring up at them. He had an engorged neck, and his mouth and nose were full of foam. The sight was somehow a little less gruesome, with the layer of frost covering everything.

"When was this guy last seen alive?" Mac asked.

Nodding, Danny said, "About three weeks ago. I checked, and it would have been a couple of days before your team identified Evan Brown as the killer."

"Good. I was concerned there was someone else killing like this."

"No. I think this was Evan. Did he freeze any of the others?" Danny asked.

Shaking her head, Mac answered, "No. There must have been something specific about this guy to make him do that."

Amanda added, "It's like he planted a time bomb, planning for it to go off just as things were getting back to normal."

Turning, Mac said as she walked away, "Yeah, one final gift from Evan."

Chapter 65

ONE YEAR LATER

BRIAN CONNOR SAT ON THE WARM SAND ON A SUNNY BEACH IN Cancún, Mexico, with a half-full drink in his hand. He was staying at a beautiful resort with great food and perfect weather, but he was still as depressed as he'd been for many months. He'd spent some time here trying to make sense of his life.

His being paroled from prison had little value without his family, and he spent several hours each day crying uncontrollably.

The inability to manage his emotions was one of the consequences of the mild brain damage he'd suffered in the near drowning. Other things were off, too, but he couldn't explain what they were. Things just weren't right in his head, and he knew it.

Tomorrow would be the one-year anniversary of the death of his son, and he felt a growing compulsion to understand why his precious son, Blake, had ended up the way he did.

One way or another, he needed answers. That might be the only thing to make him feel like himself again.

As he sat in the sun, he watched other tourists walk by, enjoying the majesty of the beach and ocean.

Eventually, a family of four walked past. There was a mom and dad and two kids, a boy and a girl. The kids were close to the ages Blake and Cindy had been when he'd gone to prison.

They were perfect, and Brian stood to follow them. He carried his small backpack that contained two cans of spray foam and a Taser pistol.

One way or another, he would understand his son.

Epilogue
14 YEARS LATER

DOCTOR STEVEN CABLE WALKED THROUGH THE MAIN DOOR AT the Pima County Adult Detention Center.

"Morning, Doc," an employee said.

Steven raised his right hand in acknowledgment.

In his left hand, he carried two case files, both of which he'd spent more than an hour reviewing early this morning.

He held up the laminated card he wore around his neck for the receptionist to see. She pressed a button, and the security lock released, allowing him past the first of several doors.

A sheriff's deputy met him, and Dr. Cable handed over the files and emptied his pockets before passing through a metal detector.

He'd brought very little in with him, knowing what was permitted and what was restricted. Besides his ID and case files, he had only a small digital voice recorder.

"You're all set, Doc," the deputy said as he returned the items.

"Thanks, Dan."

Another steel door opened, and Steven followed the familiar route to the interview room. There were two inmates he planned to speak with today as he attempted to determine their mental fitness to stand trial.

Entering the room, he sat at the plain steel table, which was bolted to the floor, and opened the first file.

Reviewing the notes, he saw that the inmate was 19 years old and had a lengthy mental health history.

In her teens, she'd run away from home, spent time in several psychiatric instructions, and been arrested for drug possession a few times.

As he reread the notes about the trauma that seemed to have started her problems, the door opened, and a thin woman in an orange jumpsuit with shackles on her wrists shuffled in.

She had a lost and distant expression on her face. Her eyes were hollow and sad, and there was bruising on her face around her left eye.

She didn't look directly at the psychiatrist but slowly moved to the chair and took a seat. Without being asked, she placed her shackled wrists on the table so the deputy who accompanied her could connect them to the metal ring built into the tabletop.

After starting the audio recorder, Steven said, "I'm Doctor Cable. The court has asked me to determine if you have the mental ability to stand trial."

The woman said nothing but nodded slightly.

"I see here that you have a long psychiatric and criminal history that leads back to your childhood."

The statement took her back to her father's death and how everything had changed, but she remained silent.

Dr. Cable noticed a single tear in the woman's eye.

"Three nights ago, you were arrested for attempted murder. Your victim fought back and escaped, but not until after you'd stabbed him."

She said nothing.

"Is that how you got the black eye?"

The woman nodded.

"Did you know the man?"

The inmate shook her head.

"So you attacked a complete stranger with a hunting knife?"

She nodded again.

"Isn't that what happened to your father? A stranger killed him."

There was no response.

"When the police searched your apartment, they found some disturbing and detailed drawings you'd made. They depict the killing of several different people. Can you explain why you drew them?"

At the mention of the drawings, the dead look in Ashley Conway's eyes was momentarily replaced with excitement as she thought about all she'd done.

The sweet young pre-schooler had grown up, but the damage from that fateful day had remained.

About the Author

 I grew up in Cape Cod, Massachusetts, and moved to Michigan in 1988 to attend Davenport University's Paramedic school. I reside in Kent City, Michigan, with my wife of 30 years. We have a son in college and an adult daughter who graduated college and lives out of town.

I am a retired firefighter/paramedic who works full-time in information systems for a major West Michigan company.

In my off time, I enjoy traveling to unique places, family time and my two dogs, who keep life fun.

———

To learn more about Christopher Coates and discover more Next Chapter authors, visit our website at www.nextchapter.pub.

A Brother's Obsession
ISBN: 978-4-82417-061-3

Published by
Next Chapter
2-5-6 SANNO
SANNO BRIDGE
143-0023 Ota-Ku, Tokyo
+818035793528

28th February 2023

CPSIA information can be obtained
at www.ICGtesting.com
Printed in the USA
LVHW101944270323
742731LV00021B/822